40hrs With A Stranger

It's a Vibe, Book I

40HRS WITH A STRANGER

BY: J.D. SOUTHWELL

Dedication

To all those who've decided to pick up this book,
thank you for giving my words a chance.

40hrs With A Stranger Playlist!

Apple Music:

Spotify:

Enjoy the playlist created for 40hrs With A Stranger.

I do not own the rights to this music.

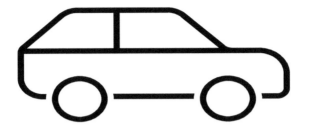

Chapter 1

Ashlynn

I covered my mouth and let out a yawn followed by a fake moan as Bobby lazily flicked his tongue against my walls. I hated when I had to beg for sex and when I finally got some, it was half-assed and boring. Ugh! I could've stuck with my damn vibrator – at least it would've had my toes curling and gripping the sheets within a matter of minutes. Hell, the synthetic tongue definitely wouldn't be missing my entire clit.

"Damn you're fucking wet," Bobby said shoving a finger inside of me.

I rolled my eyes. He must be mistaking my sweet juices for his spit because his trash ass cunnilingus was not turning me on. I let out another phony groan, feeling tired of this charade. You'd think after being in a relationship for two years, your partner would know how to please you but alas, here I was, faking.

He thrust another finger inside me, and my body jolted up. He motioned his fingers to imitate 'come here' and I began to squirm.

Finally, he was doing something that I liked. I licked my lips and gazed down at him. "Shit, that feels so good!"

He pulled his fingers out of me leaving me irritated again. Just when it was getting good, he ruined it. Bobby got up and hovered over me with his hard dick in his hands. His topaz eyes bore into me as his lips displayed a half-smile.

I looked at him and took in his delectable mocha body. He wasn't athletic, but he made a habit of playing basketball at the local rec center every weekend which kept him in shape. His dark hair was neatly shaved to a fade and his goatee was shaped to perfection. My man was absolutely fine. I reached for him, but he moved backward.

"What's wrong baby?"

"Ashlynn, I already know what you're trying to do. You want to make this a whole night extravaganza. It's already after nine and we both have to be up early for work - let's get our nut and go to bed." He said with a bit of irritation.

As I mentioned before, we had been together for two years, and last spring we got engaged. One would think our bedroom activity would be mind-blowing and non-stop. Well according to our sex lives and the bullshit that just came out of Bobby's mouth, we might as well as have been together for over twenty years - we were already burned out of each other.

When sex was involved, it was the same routine – he'd poorly give me head before shoving his dick inside me. Every now and then he'll let me give him head or get on top, but I had to make sure my sexual needs were fulfilled first. He had no restraint when I was in control and within five minutes, I easily had him cumming. Of course, I'm super proud of being able to please my man, but whenever he nutted before I was satisfied, I was shit out of luck because sexy time would be over, and he'd be fast asleep.

I sighed and nodded. Bobby got positioned in between my legs and shoved himself inside me. After about seven minutes - right on queue - Bobby's eyes began to roll to the back of his head as his back hunched.

"Gotdamn!" He groaned, his body spasming with release.

"Good job baby," I sighed sarcastically as he rolled off of me and plopped down on the bed.

"Don't start Lynn. I told you it was already late, and you know you got some good good. I can't hold my nut back especially when I'm pressured to dick you down."

I was in no mood to argue. We were having such a great week, and I did not want to start off our Friday on a bad note. It'd do nothing but cause our weekend to be full of tension and silent treatments.

"I'm good babe, really. I'm just going to take a shower," I said leaning over to kiss him. He grunted and drifted off to sleep.

I walked over to our conjoined bathroom and turned on the shower. Quietly opening the bottom cabinet, I pulled out the feminine box I kept toward the back. Instead of it holding my pads, my waterproof ten-speed vibrator sat inside. Velvet was my favorite toy because it vibrated against my clit while simultaneously thrusting against my G-spot. Not to mention, it was quieter than Big Daddy, my 10-inch toy in my top drawer.

I looked at myself in the mirror and sighed. My honey brown eyes roamed down my size eighteen pear-shaped body and rich tawny skin. My DDD-cup breasts were full but not perky. I learned at a young age that I was blessed with size and not support so I had to keep a bra on whenever I walked out of my house. I ran my hand down my cushy stomach and couldn't help but grimace.

I've always had a problem with my weight thanks to my borderline PCOS – Polycystic Ovary Syndrome – condition. I was on a constant and failing regimen. I'd workout three to five days a week for about forty-five minutes and change my eating habits. My weight would start dropping and my confidence would be boosted. Even Bobby would notice and have his hands all over me. Unfortunately, the minute I ate something high in carbs and sugar, BAM. I gained the weight back.

I shook my head and peeled off my black sheer nightgown. I was not about to trap myself into a depressive state thinking about my weight. At the end of the day, I had Bobby who loved me and we were getting married. What more could I ask for?

I made sure my hair was securely wrapped in a shower cap before stepping in the shower. I had completed my second session of heat training my hair so that it could stay straight, and I'd be damned if I got it wet. Don't get me wrong, I loved my natural curls but I had been practicing different styles on my hair for my cosmetology courses. I closed my eyes letting the hot water submerge me.

I told myself that I was content with my life right now. Outside of the unfulfilling sex and dead-end job as an accountant, I was hopeful. I had plans in place to make Bobby and I's life more exultant, starting with planning a wonderful extravagant wedding. Then, once I completed my courses and retrieved my cosmetology license, I was going to open my own hair salon.

I placed my foot on top of the garden tub side and slid Velvet right to my spot. I closed my eyes and fantasized about the future. Being a successful business owner, a happy in love wife, and getting myself permanently healthy had my toes curling and sending me to my much-needed climax.

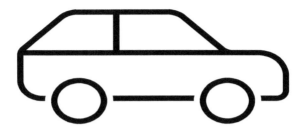

Chapter 2

Nicholas

I pressed my two fingers against my lips and placed them on top of the tombstone. The cool fall air breezed through my short freeform locs, causing me to stuff my hands back into my jacket. I didn't cry whenever I visited my brother anymore, but the pain was still there. He was the first best friend I had, and he watched over me when our parents were too doped up to care.

I felt my phone vibrate in my back pocket and contemplated on whether to ignore it. I figured it was either my mom asking for yet another handout to get her "medicine" or it was the realtor begging for me to go over the contracts to put our house up on the market while it was hot.

My brother and I had shared a three-bed and two-and-a-half-bathroom two-story home in a cozy cul-de-sac. Once we were old enough and had the down payment money together, we got out of our dangerous drug invested neighborhood and never looked back. I remember when the realtor showed us the house, we knew then it was where we were going to change our lives for the better.

My phone buzzed again in my pocket. I mumbled a curse under my breath as I fumbled to get the phone out. A small grin formed at the corner of my lips and my irritation immediately vanished when I saw Ayzo's name pop up on my screen.

I met Ayzo in my junior year in high school. He was a half Asian half Black kid who had just moved to Philly with his dad from Chicago after his mom had left them. He had short curly brown hair that went just past his eyes, golden coffee-colored skin, and almond-shaped brown eyes. He was about my height, but slimmer and already had a few tattoos that made me envious.

When Ayzo and I met for the first time outside the rec center, he told me he was an only child, and spent the majority of his time alone since his dad was always working. We became good friends – hell he became my second brother. It broke my heart when he had to go into hiding and it hurt even more that he missed the funeral. I sighed. Who am I kidding? I may have been upset, but I would've rather had him be alive and miss the funeral than have him stay in town and be buried next to my brother. I patted my brother's tombstone and turned to leave as I answered the phone.

"Look what the muthafuckin cat dragged in! Where yo ugl-ass been?"

"Haha, what's up bro? You know my ass had to lay low for a while and stay out of trouble." Ayzo chuckled through the phone. He let out a melancholy sigh and lowered his voice. "Look, I'm sorry about Garret."

"Don't," I said, cutting him off.

Silence fell through the phone for a moment as I ran my hand across the back of my neck and swore. I wasn't trying to be a complete ass to one of my oldest friends, but I seriously did not want to bring down the mood.

I cleared my throat, "I apologize Ayzo. I know you were just trying to be a good friend, but honestly, I don't want to talk about what happened right now."

"No sweat man. So," Ayzo's voice chippered back up, "the reason I called yo black ass is because I'm officially back in town. Well, not officially, I'm just visiting before I head back home to Vegas."

"Man, you ain't talking about getting fucked up tonight at Jill's," I teased pulling my car keys out of my pocket.

"Damn, Jill's still be lit like that? I thought the thrill would've died off after we all stopped going."

"C'mon man, it's a pool hall with cheap ass drinks. Of course, people still going to come through. Plus, everybody loves Ms. Jill's mean old ass and supports her especially since she lost her husband earlier this year."

"Damn, Benny gone?"

"Yes sir – died while he was dicking her down."

"Whew! That's the way to go man. Live a long life and go out deep in some pussy. Oops, may he rest peacefully with God." Ayzo said, cutting his laugh short. "Anyway, let's meet there at seven. Hopefully, there's still some fine women in there. I'm ready to find my queen."

I let out a disgusted scoff, "Man, females ain't good for nothing but getting your dick wet."

Ayzo let out a loud breath. "I forgot you were on that bullshit. All I'm going to say is leave the past in the past - don't let the hurt someone put you through yesterday, affect the new day that some people didn't get blessed to see."

"Okay Deacon Ayzo, I'll catch you later." I hung up the phone and tossed it in the passenger side of my truck.

I didn't care what Ayzo was talking about, nor did I want to hear his sermon about 'when a man findeth a good woman'. I was dead serious about how I felt about any type of female - they couldn't be trusted. If it wasn't for backstabbing women, my brother would still be alive.

I punched the air and slammed my hands against the hood of my truck. My blood boiled with the mere thought of that treacherous bitch. I caught a glimpse of myself in my truck's reflection and frowned.

I had lost weight. My once stocky 220 build dwindled to a mere 170 pounds over the course of a year. My bright hazel eyes were heavy with bags and a bit dim. The once vibrant glow that naturally radiated off my dark coco skin now had a gloomy hue. I scratched my chin and sneered - my beard needed to be trimmed and my frizzy ass locs needed to be retwisted asap so I wouldn't look like a damn bum.

I needed to get my shit together, but it was hard. I was betrayed by the woman I planned to marry and lost my best friend within the blink of an eye. I wouldn't even know where to begin for me to move on with my life, but I know one thing. I'll never allow a woman to come close to me again.

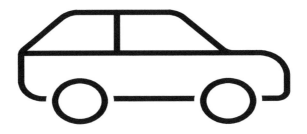

Chapter 3

Ashlynn

I rolled over and reached for Bobby but found myself touching his pillow. I looked over my shoulder to the clock on our nightstand and 8 a.m. was displayed in bold neon red. Bobby would be pulling into one of the facilities he manages about now.

My father owned a chain of 'We Got Tires' tire shops across north Philly. Bobby was the assistant manager for one of them when we first met. The store was doing so well and had such a tremendous number of excellent reviews that my father promoted him to general manager. He was in charge of making all five of my father's shops function the exact same way with similar productivity and reviews.

The amount of income and positive feedback my father received from all of Bobby's hard work with the shops made it easy for my dad to accept him as my fiancé. Hell, I'm sure he still would've been a part of my family regardless of if we were engaged or not. My dad absolutely adored Bobby.

I sighed. If only he were proud of me the same way. I spent years trying to get his approval, but it was never enough. When I graduated a year early from high school, my dad complained that I should've been the valedictorian. When I maintained my 4.0 GPA all four years of college, he made comments that I should've been number one on the Dean's list. Mind you, I was on the list, but I wasn't specifically number one. I graduated top of my class with a bachelor's degree in business and - you guessed it – he lectured that I should've obtained my master's.

To be fair, my dad wasn't always this tough on me. When my mom and grandma were alive, he did push me to better myself, but in a gentler way. I believe my mom balanced him out and my grandma, his mom, was his voice of reason. Unfortunately, when they died, balance and reasoning died within him. He became distant except for when he was criticizing me about my grades.

Once I hit puberty and started to gain weight, best believe he bluntly expressed his feelings. I swear that man did not know how to balance between blunt honesty and gentle concern. I sighed. It was hard losing mom and grandma and I missed them every day. But, it was even harder having to deal with my dad.

I huffed out a loud breath before swinging my legs off the side of the bed and standing up with a stretch. It was a new beautiful day, and I did not want to start it off depressed. Besides, since I only worked part-time as an accountant and was off today, I decided to visit my happy place, Unique's – a hair salon ran by Roshanda who also taught my night cosmetology class. She allowed me to shampoo her client's hair and shadow her while I was still learning.

I've always been fascinated with hair and wanted to be a beautician for a while now, but I had to do it secretly. Hell, I even had to hide it from Bobby because he would've told my dad. If my dad ever found out I was 'wasting my degree' – his words not mine - working at a salon, he'd have a baby cow.

My dad ultimately wanted me to join the family business so that Bobby and I could be a power couple with a nationwide chain of tire shops. Unfortunately, I had absolutely no desire for tires.

Don't get me wrong, it was a cool idea but if I fully followed along with his goals, I'd be miserable. So, until I had the balls to start my own company or until my dad was senile enough that he wouldn't notice I had my own salon, I was going to continue to follow my dreams in silence.

I finished getting ready and made sure our two-bed two-bathroom townhouse was spotless before heading out the door. I pulled into the hair salon about twenty minutes later and was about to go in when my phone rang.

"I'm surprised you two are even up this early," I said, looking at my two best friends Denice and Kendra on Facetime.

"Girl don't remind me! I'm only up because Little Miss Pre-plan everything wanted to get our weekend scheduled," Kendra said taking a sip out of her coffee mug.

Kendra worked as a bartender at a local pool hall called Jill's. She only liked working the night shifts because she said that's when she got the best tips and I one hundred percent believed her. Her energetic vibe made it easy to like her. She loved meeting new people and being the center of attention.

If her liveliness didn't grab your attention, then her beauty did. She was absolutely stunning with her smooth chestnut complexion, full lips, and petite frame. She wasn't as top heavy as I was, but she had an ass that grabbed anybody's attention. Hell, if I were single and it was my first time meeting her at the bar, I'd gladly give her my money.

"Well excuse me for wanting our best friend to have a stress-free wedding," Denice said, rolling her eyes.

Denice was the complete opposite of Kendra. She was an introvert and stayed to herself. Don't get me wrong, she liked to go out every now and then, but you'd mostly catch her at a bookstore or library buried in smutty books. That's right - she may seem quiet and innocent on the outside, but my girl had some kinks that made me blush. Her adorable girl next door vibe kept her secret hidden perfectly.

I remember running into her at our college library. Kendra and I were working on a group project when I saw her sitting alone. She was quite stunning with her thick natural curls and brown sugar complexion. Her auburn eyes danced excitedly along the lines of a biochemistry textbook, but when I looked closer, she had a copy of Zane's Addicted hidden in between the pages.

"I remember reading that in middle school," I said.

She must've not heard me walking up because she ended up dropping her cup of tea - mid sip - down the front of her white shirt and onto the table. I scrambled out of my jacket and handed it to her. Luckily, we wore the same size clothes. Kendra had witnessed the incident and was instantly on crowd control. She distracted the others in our area while we cleaned up before anyone else noticed and the librarian knew what was happening. Since then, we've all been best friends.

"Girls don't fight. Denice, I love you for helping out, but I know Kendra probably had a long night. So, let's meet up for lunch at our favorite hoagie spot."

"That works for me," Kendra said yawning.

"Me too," Denice stated with a tight lip grin.

I blew them both kisses before hanging up. Something seemed a bit off with Denice, but I knew if I pried into her business, she'd only shut down on me. Hopefully, she and Kendra weren't getting into it again – I was in no mood to deal with that type of stress.

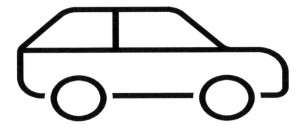

Chapter 4

Nicholas

I opened and balled my hands into fists as I took in deep breaths. I watched my mom shamelessly flirt with T, a ruthless drug dealer I used to associate with back in the day. Not by choice of course, but because of my fucking mother.

Our mother introduced us to him when I was eight and my brother was ten. I remembered him standing in the middle of our living room when we got home from school. He had on a black tracksuit with white forces and held a stuffed Nike backpack. His gold chain matched the Rolex on his wrist and the grill he had on the bottom row of his mouth. He reeked of cologne and weed that made my nose burn. He towered over us, glaring with his black eyes before arching an eyebrow at my mom. She assured him we could get the job done. Shortly after, he had us working for him.

At the time, I didn't think anything of it. T would give us little bags of weed to drop off to people in the neighborhood - hell, most of them were the parents of some of our classmates. In exchange, he'd buy us new clothes, keep food in the house for us, or just throw us a couple of twenty-dollar bills. Shit, I thought I was living the best life, but all things that glitter aren't gold.

I jumped out of my car and stormed toward my mom.

"Oh shit, little Nicholas all grown up," T laughed as he took a drag from his cigarette.

"Mom, let's go," I said, reaching for her.

"My handsome boy. Did you get my text? My lights are going to be turned off if I don't pay them and I don't have any money." She slurred, stumbling toward me and hitting the ground.

I glared down at her as she slowly picked herself back up. My nostrils flared causing my upper lip to curl at the pungent odor of weed and semen radiating off of her. My stomach churned as my eyes caught the white foam edging at the corners of her mouth.

She brushed off the dirt that stained her loose and backwards floral dress. Her hooded eyes found mine as she gave me a toothy grin. Well, it wasn't much since she'd already lost forty percent of her teeth. I frowned. The sickly thin woman with matted dark hair and dull ashen skin that stood in front of me was a complete stranger now.

I thought back to my real mother – before she got hooked on drugs. When she was sober, she was gorgeous. Her salt and pepper hair was still full and thick and sat at the top of her shoulders. Her chocolate skin was free from wrinkles beside the ones at the corner of her eyes and the corners of her mouth. She was taller than most women which complimented her small frame.

I hated when my friends saw her or when she would take me to the barbershop when I was growing up because they always made vulgar comments about how wide her hips were. I found myself in countless fights until I figured out what type of woman she was and the things she did for her daily fix.

"I told your mom I'd be more than happy to help remedy her situation," T said, a sly smile spreading across his face.

I grabbed my mom's arm and dragged her to my truck, ignoring her protests to stay with T. If I stayed a second longer, things were going to end with one of us dead. At this point in my life, I didn't care which one it would be.

"Are you going to get me the money?" she asked, leaning against my truck.

"Hell no, now get in," I snapped, opening the door behind her. Her eyes furrowed in confusion as she looked up at me. I pulled her toward the door, but she planted her feet waiting for an explanation. I sighed and rubbed the bridge of my nose. "Look, I know for a fact your ass don't need money to pay any kind of bills because I made sure everything was paid up for the next couple of months."

Her mouth opened and then closed again. A look of grief cast on her face for a brief moment as her eyes looked everywhere but at me. I felt bad for her and wanted her to be my mom again before she got hooked on these drugs. For the first seven years of my life, she was a completely different woman. She was loving, kind, funny, and lively but when our dad left, she searched for a coping mechanism. Unfortunately, she chose the wrong one.

"Okay fine," she said stomping her foot, "I want some spending money."

"For what?"

"That's none of your damn business boy," she snapped, pointing a finger at me.

"Ma, you have food, clothes, and a roof over your head. What else could you possibly need?"

"I have hobbies Nicholas. Maybe I want to go play bingo with my friends or start a damn stamp collection. I mean who gives a fuck! I need money and it's not right that you have all of it."

"It's not right?" I yelled back at her.

"Yes! It's not right that you have all of the life insurance from Garrett just sitting in your bank account. Dammit, he was my son, and it belongs to me. How much was it anyway?"

I stared at her in disbelief. She'd been hounding me about not being the beneficiary for Garrett's life insurance policy ever since he died. I swore she was more upset that she didn't have the money than actually losing him.

"Ma, get in the fucking truck so I can take you home. You don't need shit especially not from T's bitch ass. If you want extra money, then sober the fuck up and get a fucking job."

"Don't talk to me like that! I am your mother!"

"You stopped being my mother the day you whored yourself to crack!" I roared. My head snapped to the side as her hand struck my cheek.

"Get out of here Nicholas. I'll find my own way home," she whispered.

I glared as I watched her turn on her heels and stagger away. I contemplated going after her but decided not to – there wasn't a point. Fuck her! I spat on the ground. I was through helping her ass. I looked down at my watch and saw it was a quarter past twelve. I needed a drink.

.

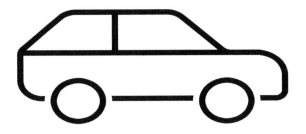

Chapter 5

Nicholas

I grabbed a bottle of whisky, and a can of soda before standing in line. The usual cashier, Mr. Jimmy, wasn't there today, but some woman was there instead. She had to be a bit younger than me – probably in her late twenties - with long red hair and matching acrylic nails. She had on a dark gray crop top hoodie that showed off her mid-drift and matching sweatpants. She was cute with her warm caramel skin and full lips. I cocked my head to the side to see her perky C-cup breasts and juicy ass. Not bad.

The line began to move and as I got closer, I started to realize I knew the woman behind the counter. I licked my lips and approached the counter when it was finally my turn. She reached for the items I sat down while nonchalantly scrolling through her phone. I exaggeratedly cleared my throat. She rolled her eyes and sat her phone down, but her annoyance quickly dissolved when she locked eyes with me. Her deep brown eyes lit up and a smile formed across her face.

"Well, I be damned, Charity. I haven't seen you around here in a minute," I said smiling at her.

"Why, hello Nicholas," she said, beaming back at me. "How have you been doing?" she asked.

She graduated a few years after I did, and we had a few mutual friends. I always used to think she was fuckable but didn't pursue anything with her.

"I'm good. Where's Mr. Jimmy?"

"My uncle was running late and asked me to open up shop for a little bit," she cooed running her pierced tongue across her bottom lip as her eyes drifted up and down my body. I felt my dick press against my pants. "I was hoping to run into you one of these days. You know I used to have the biggest crush on you."

"Is that right?" I asked, staring into her brown eyes.

"Hell yeah! You've always been sexy as fuck, and I used to wonder what you'd taste like."

I rubbed my beard and chuckled. "Last I heard, you were engaged – as soon as you graduated right?"

She sighed, "Yeah, I got married. Young and dumb, but now he spends more time with his mistress than he does with me. Why does he have to be the only one getting his needs met?"

I arched my eyebrow as I handed her my card to pay for my items. She took it but let her fingers brush against my hand. She stared at my lips as she bit onto hers and slowly made eye contact with me. She was shamelessly undressing me with her eyes.

She jumped slightly when the back door opened and slammed shut, realizing her uncle had made it in when he coughed. She winked at me and finished ringing up my items before handing me back my debit card.

"Hey Mr. Jimmy, how's it going?" I said, breaking my gaze with Charity.

"Ahh young blood, another day another dollar," he said, walking behind the counter. He gave me a handshake before sitting down at his usual spot. "Charity baby, thank you for helping your uncle out, but you can head out."

"You sure Unc? I can stay and help you a bit longer?"

"Nah sweetheart you've done enough. Besides Jackie will be here in an hour to start her shift."

"Okay call me if you need me," she said kissing him on the cheek.

She disappeared to the back toward the employee area. I talked to Mr. Jimmy for a bit before gathering my things and heading out the door. When I got to my truck, Charity was standing there.

"My place is just up the block," she said.

I opened the bottle of whisky and took a long swig before nodding at her. I opened the passenger door watching as she climbed in. I only wanted a damn drink, but shit if she wanted to get fucked, I wasn't going to protest.

Within ten minutes we pulled into her apartment complex and reached her front door. She giggled and tried to kiss me, but I dodged her. I didn't do that kissing shit, but I turned her around and trailed my tongue up the back of her neck as she fumbled with her keys instead. I ran my hands up the front of her crop top and squeezed her breast.

"I love how rough you are," Charity purred.

"Open the door so I can show you how rough I can be," I snarled in her ear.

She let out a whimper and finally got the door open. I gently shoved her inside and closed the door, bolting it behind me.

"You ready for me sexy?" she asked wrapping her arms around me and resting her chin on my back.

I turned to face her, grabbing her hips and pulling her closer to me "Don't talk, just strip." I demanded.

She giggled and pulled me toward her bedroom. She wasted no time by pushing me onto the bed and doing exactly what I instructed. She yanked her hoodie over her head and dropped her sweatpants revealing her sheer red bra and matching panties.

Hmph, interesting. She must've had a plan to get into bed with the first man who got her panties wet, just to get back at her husband. It's not like I've never seen a woman wear sexy ass lingerie but under her regular clothes? I don't think so! Not unless she planned to get dicked down. Oh, well. I honestly didn't care – shit, I was only here to relieve some stress, not to pursue a damn relationship.

She walked over to me, unbuckled my belt, and jerked off my pants, leaving me in my boxers. I reached up and bit her nipple through her bra. She moaned as she pulled my shirt up over my head. The wet heat radiating between her legs had my dick ready to slide in between her.

I reached around and unhooked her bra freeing her scrumptious breasts. Her nipples instantly hardened as I sucked them into my mouth.

"Mmmm," she moaned as she grinded her hips against me. She leaned down and licked my neck. I slapped her on her ass, making her giggle in my ear. I pulled her hips closer to mine and dug myself against her. Her eyes widened with the realization of how thick I was and need instantly filled her eyes.

She slid off me and crawled down to the bottom of the bed to her knees. She pulled out my dick and slowly slid her tongue up my length. I let out a groan as the metal ball pierced into her tongue brushed against me. I gripped her head as she sucked me entirely into her mouth.

"Spit on that shit," I demanded.

She obeyed, getting my dick sloppily wet. My eyes rolled to the back of my head with each stroke of her tongue. After a few moments, I pulled her up and pushed her onto her back. I kicked her legs apart with my knees as I licked from her ears down to her navel. Her body shuddered and her back arched.

"Oh baby!" she moaned. I watched her body squirm underneath me as I pulled her panties to the side and rubbed my thumb against her clit. I inserted a finger deep inside her as she bucked against me.

"Stop teasing and fuck me!" She cried out as she grinded against my fingers.

I licked my lips – she was so wet and ready for my dick. I reached down and pulled a condom out of my pocket when I felt her hand grab my wrist.

"You don't need that baby. I'm clean."

"I don't play about my health," I said, removing her hand.

I moved out of reach as I slipped the condom on. I didn't care how fine and wet she was, I was not about to jeopardize a lifetime of health issues for a brief moment of pleasure, nor was I going to be trapped into being somebody's baby daddy. She clenched her jaw before nodding and pulling her panties off.

I placed one of her long legs onto my shoulders as I guided my dick to her opening. She gasped as I promptly stretched and filled her. I alternated between long deep strokes and short fast ones.

"Aww fuck Nicholas, "Charity cried as she squeezed her breast. I watched with fascination as her eyes rolled to the back of her head with each climatic release I gave her.

"Take this dick," I demanded as I pounded into her harder. The mixture of her headboard banging against the wall and the sounds of her moans, was driving me crazy.

Not wanting to cum yet, I rolled to my back and had her ride my dick. I held one hand onto her hips and the other on her breast as she bounced up and down. The urge to nut became harder to hold back as she grinded her pussy against me. I grabbed her hips and thrust myself deep inside her causing her head to fall back as she moaned. I felt a flutter in the pit of my stomach as my balls tightened.

"Fuck!" I groaned as I felt my nut fill up the condom.

She dropped to the bed next to me and nothing but the sounds of us catching our breaths filled the room. After a few moments, I sat up and gathered my clothes.

"Where are you going?" she asked, gazing up at me.

"Why?"

"I can't ask?"

I exhaled loudly. "About to go handle some business."

Pulling my pants up, I grabbed my phone and texted my barber to see if he could line me up. I also made sure one of his female hair-stylists were available to retwist my locs.

"I feel you. I need to get up and go pay some of my bills before I get thrown out of here," she paused and stared at me. She chewed her bottom lip and twirled her thumbs. "So, uh, do you think you can help me out?"

"What?" I said, glaring down at her.

"I gave you some pussy so help me out with a couple hundred dollars so I can pay my rent. I know you got it."

"Who the fuck told you that bullshit?"

"A little birdie. I helped you so help me," she said sitting on her knees in the bed.

My stomach flipped and heat traveled to my head as anger grew through me. This bitch really thought I was going to give her some money just because she gave up some pussy. I looked at her up and down and scoffed before heading out the door. Another reason why I never trust these hoes.

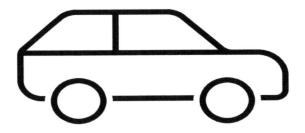

Chapter 6

Ashlynn

I walked back into my house and plopped down on the couch. Even though I was tired and in dire need of a bubble bath, I was quite proud of my accomplishments today. I had successfully completed my course and lab work for haircutting and styling at school. Roshanda allowed me to practice on her hair and was proud of my excellent work. All I had to do now was prepare for my cosmetology license exam. Maybe then, I'd tell my dad my dream of opening up my own salon.

"Yeah right," I laughed out loud, "Like Dad would allow that."

My phone rang in my purse and nervousness hit the pit of my stomach when I saw my dad's name displayed on the screen. Ugh, he must've had a microphone hidden somewhere because every time I mentioned him, he called. I took a breath and put on a smile before answering the phone.

"Hey, Dad! How's it going in Cali?"

"It's fast. Everybody is in such a damn rush over here, not that I am complaining,"

I laughed and rolled my eyes because he literally was. "C'mon Dad, you said you wanted to expand your company more and you're in a great place to do so."

"Yeah yeah, I know. Anyways, I have a bit of news to tell you." He let out a loud sigh and swallowed. "Your grandpa isn't doing so well."

My heart thumped loudly, and panic swelled in my throat. "What? What's going on?"

"Well long story short, they found cancer. The doctors are still doing some tests, but they said the survival rate of this type of cancer is less than seven percent."

"Oh my God," I whispered. I attempted to swallow the lump in my throat but failed miserably. Within seconds, uncontrollable tears streamed down my cheek.

"I know baby girl - you and your grandpa were always close. Hell, you were closer to him than me, so I know how hard this news is to hear. I bet if it were vice versa, you wouldn't be this upset."

I shook my head in disbelief and sniffed. "Dad, seriously? You aren't possibly using this time to throw jealousy in my face?"

"I'm just stating facts. I never had the chance to build a tight bond with you and I'm your damn dad."

"Because you made unnecessarily mean comments about my grades, my goals, and even my weight. Hell, you pushed me and paw-paw away after Mom -," my voice trailed off as I swiped away the tears.

My dad sighed sarcastically, "I'm sorry I wanted you to be successful in life so that you can obtain a sensible and profitable career. And kids are mean! I didn't want you to be bullied at school for being overweight."

"So, being a bully at home was what? Motivation for me to lose weight so I didn't have to be picked on at school?"

"Don't be so sensitive Ashlynn - I just wanted you to be healthy and happy. Your mom would've wanted the same thing."

I closed my eyes and exhaled. There was no point in arguing with this man – when he said he was right, then that was all there was to it. "Look, I am going to come over there to visit…the both of you. I can catch a flight Sunday morning."

"That won't be enough time for Bobby to get his affairs in order at the shops." My dad protested.

I rolled my eyes. He didn't care to ask about my job security but then again, since I wasn't working for his business, he didn't care.

"I'm sure it'll be fine. If anything, he'll catch a later flight and meet me there."

My phone buzzed with a text notification from Denice asking if Kendra and I were available to jump on a Facetime call.

"Dad, I'm going to have to let you go. I'm meeting up with my friends to start looking for my wedding dress."

He grunted and mumbled something under his breath.

"What?" I asked, irritated.

"Well, I thought you said you wanted to lose more weight before you officially went dress shopping. You know a lot of those shops don't carry dresses your size."

"Okay, thanks, Dad. I'll talk to you later. Love you," I didn't bother to listen if he responded back and hung up the phone.

My blood boiled as anger washed over me. Why was he so obsessed with my damn weight? I mean sure he wanted me to be healthy, but why did he have to bring it up every chance he got? Why couldn't he just love me the way I was?

Bile rushed up my throat and I ran to the hall bathroom. I didn't eat much throughout the day except for a few carrots and a kid size hoagie with the girls but it came right up. When I thought I was done, I shoved my finger down my throat and puked some more.

For the past two years, I've been making myself vomit or pushing my body into starvation which helped me shed pounds. Even though I knew it wasn't healthy for me, it was satisfying to see the scale go down. Even if it was temporary.

I didn't consider myself to be a bulimic since I knew I could stop at any time. Well, that's what I keep telling myself, anyway. I thought about reaching out for help, but who was I kidding? No one wants to hear the sob story of an overweight black woman. So, I decided this secret was just going to stay with me – no matter how long it took for me to lose weight.

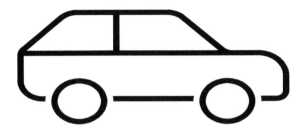

Chapter 7

Ashlynn

I ran my hands down the chiffon fabric, my fingers grazing each lace pattern. The pearly white buttons assembled midway down leaving the rest of the mannequins back exposed. The dress was beautiful and simple, but unfortunately not in my size.

"I wish you could try that dress on, it is absolutely beautiful," Kendra said, standing next to me.

"Yeah," I sighed.

"Damn I would snatch this dress up in a heartbeat!" Kendra cooed, holding the gown against her in the mirror.

"Damn Kendra!" Denice snapped, "Kick a bitch while she's down why don't you."

"My bad! I was just saying."

"It's cool but I agree, the dress is breathtaking," I said, desire gripping my throat.

"Why don't you just order a dress online? I doubt any of the shops we visit today will have your size," Kendra said half-heartedly. Denice opened her mouth to argue, but Kendra's phone began to ring. She looked down and smiled, "Excuse me, ladies."

She tossed the dress back on the rack before dashing out the door.

"I swear Kendra can be so inconsiderate sometimes," Denice mumbled, neatly putting the gown back on the rack. She looked up at me with a frown plastered on her face. "I am really sorry things are not going as planned."

"Dee don't do that. I love you for trying so hard to make my day special," I said hugging her. "Trust me I am not stressing – we'll find a beautiful wedding dress and some sexy ass bridesmaids dresses before you know it."

She smiled, but it instantly vanished. Her eyebrows furrowed together as she squinted her eyes. "What is Bobby doing here?"

"Huh? Bobby?" I asked in confusion. I turned my head to what she was looking at and lo and behold Bobby was standing against his car talking to Kendra.

"Did you know he was going to be here?" Denice asked.

"Nope. He knows it's bad luck to see the dress before the wedding." I playfully chuckled and headed toward the door. My smile staggered as Kendra laughed and ran her hand down Bobby's arm. My eyes furrowed as I stepped out of the dress shop.

"Hey Dee," Bobby said taking a few subtle steps away from Kendra. "Hey, baby."

"Bobby, what are you doing here?" I asked, looking between him and Kendra.

"I swear I didn't see any dress that may have interested you. I know your superstitious ass thinks it's bad luck."

"I was just explaining to Bobby it's tradition to not see the dress until the wedding day," Kendra said, teasingly nudging him in the arm.

I laughed, "Thank you, girl! I've been trying to explain that to him. Bobby don't worry though, you wouldn't have been able to see from here anyway."

"Were you able to try on any of the dresses you liked?" Bobby asked.

"Nope," Kendra said nonchalantly.

"Kendra!" Denice snapped glaring at her.

"What?" she said, folding her arms. "Sorry, it's the truth. Don't get pissy with me because they didn't have her size! Look, I've got to go - my shift starts later, and I want to get some sleep before I go in."

Denice shook her head and walked back inside the store.

"I'm sorry again to interrupt, but uh –" Bobby paused, watching Kendra as she walked off. "Oh, you texted something about needing to talk to me last night, but I got caught up with my work. By the time I made it back home, you were already fast asleep. Kendra said you all were meeting here to dress shop, so here I am."

"You and Kendra are texting each other?" I asked, folding my arms.

"Calm down baby, not like that! You remember that group chat you set up a while back with us? About the whole Juneteenth get to-gether?"

"Yes, but I thought it was just us girls," I stated in confusion. I scratched the side of my head and tried to recall the messages. I mean, I definitely remember setting up the party back in June – guess I forgot I added Bobby to the chat.

"Can I steal you away for a few minutes so we can talk?"

"Of course," I said snapping out of my train of thought and grabbing onto his extended arm.

I sent Denice a quick message that I was taking a quick walk with Bobby and if she didn't want to wait around, I could meet her at Brenda's Boutique in an hour. She sent back a thumbs-up emoji as we walked down South Street.

"So what was it that you needed to talk about?" Bobby asked.

"Well," I said taking a deep breath, "Grandpa has cancer and doesn't have much time left."

"Damn," Bobby muttered. We stopped walking as he embraced me, before guiding us to a nearby bench. "I'm sorry to hear that baby. How are you holding up?"

"Honestly, it hasn't registered yet. I think I am still in shock. I planned on flying out there tomorrow evening to visit for a while."

Bobby's thumbs brushed idly on the back of my hand as concern filled his eyes. "Of course, whatever you need baby. I am here to support you."

"Do you think you can fly out sometime later next week?" I asked enjoying his tender touch.

Bobby stopped caressing my hand and rubbed the back of his neck. "Bae, you know I can't just drop what I am doing to go out of town. I have too much work to do. One of the stores is going through an inspection and I need to be there to make sure -"

"Please, babe," I begged, interrupting him. "Having your love and support with not only dealing with my grandpa but also my dad would be much appreciated. Besides, you know how much my dad adores you. You'd be able to preoccupy him while I spent time with my grandpa."

Bobby gripped the bridge of his nose. "I understand, but I just can't. If anything, your dad would appreciate it if I stayed and kept his business running smoothly."

"Fine," I huffed watching the local tourists snap pictures of the scenery.

I admired them. I lived in Philly damn near my whole life and was so used to the area that I hadn't stopped to appreciate the beautiful creations that God had made. The warm tapestry of orange and yellow leaves blew carefree with the crisp wind creating a picturesque landscape. I closed my eyes and listened to the bustling city.

"Ashlynn!" Bobby snapped shaking my shoulder. "Yo, where did you go?"

"Oh sorry, just thinking. What did you say?"

He let out an aggravated sigh, "I asked you how much your plane ticket was."

"About five hundred with a twelve-hour delay. A nonstop flight is looking at close to a grand."

"Fuck!"

"Right, but it is close to Thanksgiving."

"Well, you'll have to take it out of your dress budget," Bobby said nonchalantly scrolling through his phone. "Or you could drive there."

"That's over forty hours!" I retorted, throwing my hands up.

"Don't cause a scene, Ashlynn. I'm just saying it would be cheaper to drive. I mean your car is pretty new and would make the drive easy - not to mention it has impeccable gas mileage. You'd easily save a couple of hundred dollars by driving."

"It's over forty hours," I said again through clenched teeth. "You want me to drive across the country, alone, just to save money?"

"I could care less, Ashlynn," Bobby barked, standing up. "It's your dress budget. Hell, if you worked full-time instead of that part-time bullshit, you could pay it by your damn self."

"You son of a bitch!" I yelled. I stood up from the bench and stormed back toward the boutique.

"Wait!" Bobby shouted, catching up to me. "I'm sorry. I'm just super stressed at work and bills, I just-I'm an idiot."

I folded my arms across my chest and glared at him. "How could you say something so insensitive to me?"

"You're right, I am sorry Ashlynn," he said grabbing me by the waist.

He wrapped his arms around me tightly. My shoulders sagged as I held him back and tried to hold back my tears.

"All I am saying love is to just think about it. I know it's a long drive, but it'll give you time to process everything with your grandpa and dad. I know being around them both can be extremely overwhelming, and I just thought the drive could help clear your head before you saw them."

I took in a deep breath and exhaled. He was right. No, I did not want to take that long trip on my own, but I needed the time to gather my thoughts. I wanted to be prepared to see my grandpa - Lord knows what type of condition he'd be in when I got there. I also needed to prepare to see my dad. I was going to finally tell him my goal of opening my own salon and turning down his offer to take over his business.

It was just a few days on the road, how bad could it be?

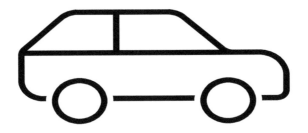

Chapter 8

Nicholas

As usual, Jill's was packed with locals and tourists, but I didn't mind, especially if it meant more income for Ms. Jill. I sat at the bar and Kendra, the bartender, sat down a double whisky on the rocks. She winked at me before walking off to assist a customer. I liked it when she worked because she knew exactly what I liked and kept my drinks coming without having to ask.

I observed around the establishment looking for Ayzo but he hadn't made it yet. The billiard tables were crowded with patrons enjoying the game as they socialized. I wanted to play but didn't like playing with people I did not know – that's how most altercations happened around here.

I stared at the walls adorned with sports mementos that Benny had collected over the years and smiled. I remembered each time he hung one up, Jill fussed at him for cluttering up her walls – but she never made him take them down.

"What's up, bro?" Ayzo said walking up to me. I stood up and hugged him.

"Man, I missed yo ugly ass," I said waving Kendra over.

"Me too man. Two years is a long time."

"What can I get for you, sweetie?" Kendra asked smiling at Ayzo.

"Is your number an option?"

Kendra laughed, "I don't know, depends."

"He'll take Patron with Sprite," I said, shutting down their flirting. Kendra arched her eyebrow at me before nodding and walking off.

"Damn man, why you blockin'?"

"Trust me, you don't want to fool with Kendra's ass. She nothing but a gold digger."

Ayzo smacked his lips, "Man how you know? Did you already hit?"

"Hell nah," I said shaking my head in disgust. "Look, she be in here bragging about all of the rich boy toys she has."

"Man, you be in here like that?"

I shook my head. "Does that matter? Besides, people tell me stuff."

"And why is that?" Ayzo laughed, gulping his drink.

"I must have an approachable face."

"And you believe what they be saying?"

"Drunk man tells no tales," I shrugged.

Ayzo waved his hand at me and smacked his lips.

"Plus, I've seen one of them in here the other night. He's quite territorial. He watched her like a damn hawk all night."

"Maybe that's their thing. You know, they little special kinky shit that gets them going in the bedroom. While she works, he acts like a stalker creep and they pretend they don't know each other."

I laughed and shook my head. "Yeah maybe. Apparently, the dude got an old lady, though."

"Ain't that about a bitch!" Ayzo scoffed, sipping his drink.

"Right! Kendra ass knows it too – let her tell it but she'll brag on that shit."

"That's cold. Alright alright! I'll leave the wicked witch alone," Ayzo said rubbing, the side of his temples. "So, what you been up to?"

"Not a damn thing," I shrugged.

"So, you've just been people watching at Jill's since the last time I saw you two years ago?"

"C'mon stop playing. I have been watching after Mom's and just going with the flow. If I can be honest with you bro, I have been stuck in this depressing rut that I can't seem to shake. It's like I am missing something, but I can't figure out what it is."

"You need a hobby – something to preoccupy your time. What happened to you getting back into music?" he asked as Kendra brought us a refill.

"Nah, I'm too old to be trying to get into the music industry. Besides, if I treated it as work, I wouldn't enjoy it anymore."

"That's true. Maybe you need to just get out of Philly for a while. Shit, after everything that went down for me, I hauled ass out of here. I have to say, it's one of the best things I've done."

I nodded and thought about traveling. I mean there's so much of the world that I haven't seen yet, but I guess I was just worried about my mom. I know she wasn't about to change, but I couldn't just leave her to the streets.

"Fuck it. I'm already in the process of selling the house – why shouldn't I move around for a bit?"

"When's the last time you've been in there?" Ayzo asked, staring at his drink.

"Not since I came back from the hospital and that was only to get some of my clothes."

He nodded and took a few gulps from his drink. "I passed by earlier today. Maybe it'll be a start to moving on for you if you just drove by."

"I can't do that man – too many painful memories."

"I understand and in no way am I telling you to do it immediately. Baby steps Nicholas." He explained patting me on the shoulder. He gave me a sympathetic grin before his phone began to vibrate against the countertop. The color from his face drained as he stared at it.

"What's wrong man?" I asked frowning.

He opened his mouth to say something but closed it. He looked up at me with deep concern as he gripped his phone. "It's uh…"

"C'mon man, you making me worried – spit it out."

"Shit," he grumbled as he downed the rest of his drink. "Okay, my homie back home Vincent was telling me about this fine ass girl he's been hooking up with."

"Okay and?"

"Well, he just showed me a picture of her," Ayzo said. He hesitated before sliding me his phone.

I looked down and my mouth flew open. I couldn't believe my fucking eyes.

"Olivia," I said through clenched teeth. I gripped my glass so hard I thought it was going to shatter in my hands.

"Look man, I get it your pissed at her, but she's out of your life now."

"Where the fuck is she?" I spat, shoving the phone into his chest. "

"Nicholas, calm down man."

"Where. Is. She?" I growled, jabbing my finger into his chest.

"Back in Vegas," he said swatting my hand away. "She lives with my homie off the strip. Look, my homeboy is a good dude and doesn't deserve your wrath."

"I'm not worried about him. I'm only after Olivia. Let's go," I said standing up.

"Go where? Back to Vegas?"

"Yes!"

"First off, my plane doesn't leave until the end of next week. Second of all, I will not participate in your crusade of rampage."

"Fine!" I barked, slamming down my money for my tab. "Send me the address to his spot."

"Are you for real?"

"Don't even worry about it. Vincent right? I'll find it!"

"Nicholas!" Ayzo shouted after me, but I didn't turn back.

I stormed out of Jill's and hopped into my truck. A part of me felt bad for abandoning Ayzo, but I needed to get to Vegas. As soon as I saw the picture of my ex, I knew exactly what I was missing in my life. I needed that bitch to pay for her sins.

I scrolled through my phone for the fastest way to Vegas. The first plane out was damn near a thousand bucks. It's not like I didn't have the money for it but fuck that. I wasn't about to throw a grand down the toilet for some economy ass seats. I thought about driving but changed my mind. I didn't not want that many miles on my truck nor was I going to drive across the country on my own.

"Fuck it," I grumbled as I purchased a bus ticket. I put my keys in the ignition and raced to the hotel I had been staying at for the past year – the bus was due to leave in a couple of hours.

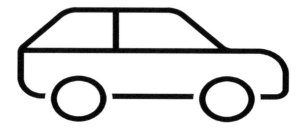

Chapter 9

Ashlynn

I lugged the last suitcase down the driveway and placed it in the trunk of my car. I cursed as I checked my Apple watch. It was just after 5 a.m. and I wanted to beat the Sunday morning drivers but was already running behind schedule. Bobby reassured me he'd have my bags in the car for me when I got home from spending time with Denice – Kendra had to work - but I was unsurprisingly disappointed.

"Hey," I said walking into the kitchen as Bobby was filling a thermal full of coffee.

"Babe, I am sorry about the suitcases. I had a bit too many last night with the boys and it slipped my mind."

"No worries, I'm just glad you made it back safely. Is that for me?"

"You betcha! Two scoops of sugar and peppermint mocha creamer, just like you like it," he said closing the lid. He placed it on the counter in front of me and wrapped his arms around my waist. "You know I would be driving with you if it wasn't for all of this work."

"I know," I said laying my head on his chest.

"You are so good to me, and I love you," he whispered in my hair before planting a kiss on my forehead.

I closed my eyes and rested there for a few moments as he rubbed his hand up and down my back. As much as I loved Bobby, I still had a nagging thought that our relationship wouldn't survive, especially not as husband and wife. I mean he worked hard to support us and took care of the majority of our bills. I trusted him and I knew how romantic he could be, but lately, something seemed off with him. He was becoming more distant and complained about how tired he was, causing our sex lives to be nonexistent. On top of that, he was starting to slide in slick comments about my weight – just like my dad.

He placed his hand under my chin and tilted my head back as he deeply kissed my lips. His hands caressed my back before he broke off our kiss and gave me a tight hug. I smiled and lightly chuckled to myself. What was I thinking? How could I doubt our future when I knew he loved me? I needed to stop being so skeptical and have faith that everything was going to work out for us.

"Oh, I forgot to tell you the shit my dad said when I talked to him. He had the nerve to ask me why I was wedding dress shopping if I hadn't lost weight."

Bobby stiffened and it seemed as if he was holding his breath. Knowing him, he was biting his tongue.

"Spit it out," I said bracing myself.

"I don't want you to get upset, but you did say you wanted to drop two sizes to fit into your wedding dress. All I'm saying is you can't really get upset with your dad when you were the one who originally said - "

I cut his sentence short by pushing off of him. "Why do you always do that?"

"Do what?"

"You always take my dad's side."

"Please don't start. You know I do not do that. All I was doing was stating facts. You said you wanted to lose weight and your dad was just reminding you of your goal. Plus, I thought going dress shopping was a good idea. Not to buy a dress of course but be a great motivator for you to look at all the potential dresses you could fit into one day. You don't want to look back at our wedding photos and get mad when you see your body ruining your dream dress," Bobby said smiling.

I didn't know if I wanted to throw the thermal of coffee at him or to knee him in the gut. Did he really think those were words of encouragement to make me feel better? I was on the verge of tears, but I had no one to blame but myself. I shouldn't have even brought it up.

"Look, the last thing I want to do is argue with you before you leave. I don't want you on the road upset or pissed off."

I dropped my arms and nodded. "It's getting late anyway, and I have to go. I'm going to run to the ladies. I left my phone charger upstairs; do you mind grabbing it for me?"

Bobby nodded and left the room. I waited a few minutes before walking into the guest bathroom and emptying my stomach by shoving my finger down my throat. I hated feeling this way and couldn't help but think if I was thinner things would be better.

I brushed my teeth with the spare brush I left under the sink and stepped on the scale watching the numbers crawl higher and higher. 245 pounds stood boldly in red at my feet. If I could just get back to 190 pounds like when Bobby and I first met, I'd be good to go.

I left the bathroom and called up the stairs.

"Don't fret my love, I placed your charger in your backpack already," Bobby called down.

"You're the best," I said grabbing the thermal. "Get some sleep, I'll call you when I make it to Columbus."

"Alright baby, I love you."

"I love you too," I said and headed out the door.

****

"That fucking idiot!" I shouted as I dumped my backpack onto the passenger side seat. I had just made it into Columbus, Ohio, and was pulled over on the Northwestern Turnpike. My phone battery had less than ten percent and I was about to charge it until I realized that

Bobby fucked up. He didn't put my phone charger in my backpack – instead, he gave me the charger for my dildo.

I slammed the passenger door shut and cursed. Looking around, I hooded my eyes with my hands to read a sign up ahead. I was about 5 miles away from the next gas station. They had to have a charger I could buy or at least guide me to the store that did. I hopped back into my car and closed my eyes. I inhaled a count of three and exhaled a few times allowing the tension in my body to ease.

"Don't panic Ashlynn. Gas stations usually have USB charging cords for iPhones, so there's no need to get all worked up. Everything's going to be okay, God's got your back" I spoke out loud as I placed the keys back into the ignition.

Within 20 minutes, I was praising the Lord as I pulled into the gas station and was able to purchase a compatible charger. I was beyond relieved even though I was way behind schedule. I plugged in the charger and attempted to start the car, but nothing happened except for a loud clicking noise. I tried turning over the ignition again while pressing the brakes, but again nothing.

"Sounds like a dead battery," an older woman said walking back to her minivan. She placed her items in the passenger seat as she climbed in. "Had it happened to me a few times. If you want, I can give you Willy Earl's number. He's a traveling mechanic that's about 45 minutes out. He does great work."

"Thanks," I said as she dialed his number for me on her phone. After a few back and forth pleasantries between the two, he agreed to be there within the hour to help me. I thanked her again as she backed out of lot leaving me, my dead car, and dead phone in the parking lot.

I punched the steering wheel a few times as I rested my back against the car. Bobby had reassured me time after time that my drive was going to be a breeze and my car was good to go. I couldn't even call to fuss at him, causing me to be even more frustrated. Ugh! I knew I should've trusted my gut to get my car checked out before I left.

"Help me Lord," I said lifting my head toward the sky.

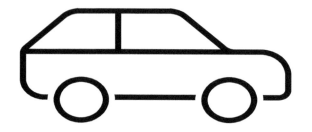

Chapter 10

Nicholas – Two Years Ago

I watched Olivia lick the paper as she rolled up her joint. Her wide hips and plump ass swayed as Ari Lennox's Shea Butter blasted through my Bluetooth speaker in my room. Her long brown curls were loosely tied up into a bun accenting her long kissable neck. She looked over her shoulder and winked at me as she grabbed a lighter out of her oversized hoodie pocket.

I sat on the bed and watched her in awe. I loved it when she wore baggy clothes, especially when they were mine. She was no taller than 5'4 and had a small frame – seeing my shirts overpower her, turned me on. It made me want to bend her over again and again, not caring about the consequences.

The first time I laid eyes on her, I just had to have her. She and her mother moved to our neighborhood my sophomore year in high school, and I was mesmerized by her beauty. I had never been with a Latina girl from the West Coast, so trying to shoot my shot with her was a challenge. She didn't tolerate the same basic bullshit that the other gullible girls in my grade did. I eventually won her over by writing her a love poem in full Spanish and we'd been together ever since.

"Mi amor, ¿que paso?" she asked, taking a puff from her blunt. "Why are you staring at me?"

"Dang, I can't stare at my fine ass woman?" I asked, placing my hand over my heart.

"I'm sorry Papi," she laughed walking over to me. She pushed me down on my back and straddled my lap. "How can I make it up to you?"

"I can think of some ways," I said licking my lips and slapping her ass.

Before I could reenact all the dirty things I was thinking, a knock came at my door. I dropped my head back and cursed.

"Dammit Garrett," I mumbled, lifting Olivia off of my lap.

"Yo you ready?" he asked as I opened my room door. "What up Liv?"

"Hey G!" she waved and took another hit from her blunt.

"You couldn't wait one more hour, could you?" I asked, annoyed.

"Sorry little bro, but I want to get this shit over with. I don't like having all this product in our house. Besides, think of it like this: once we make this drop, our mortgage will be paid off and we can officially get out of the game."

"Man, we've already been out of the game since we left Mom's," I grumbled as I grabbed my shoes out of my closet.

Leaning against the door frame, Garrett crossed his arms. He was two inches taller compared to my six foot frame and maintained his athletic build even though he hadn't played basketball since high school. He may have been two years older, but his smooth beard-free baby face begged a differ. His shoulder length dread locs were tied in a ponytail exposing a tattoo on his neck of his favorite Bible verse – Psalms 27:1. *The Lord is my light and my salvation, whom shall I fear?*

"True," Garrett said, rubbing the side of his face. "Unfortunately, after putting the down payment on this house and paying the mortgage up for the year, paying off both our cars, and managing to keep something in our savings – we could use the extra money. Once we complete this job, we'll be set for a long while. You can go invest or start your music career, or…wink wink," Garrett said darting his eyes towards Olivia.

I laughed and threw my shoe at him. I had confided in him earlier this month about how I was going to ask her to marry me on her birthday and he was failing miserably to keep it a secret from her.

"We could rent out the house and move the fuck up out of here," I said, standing up. Garrett smiled and nodded. I heaved a sigh and finished gathering my things.

Garrett had run into one of his homeboys from high school last week. He begged Garrett to help with this dangerous job promising to let us keep forty percent. Garrett had a more sympathetic heart than me because I would've told his ass to go straight to hell. I didn't trust a word half these muthafuckas said, especially since he wasn't close family like Ayzo and Olivia. However, I wasn't going to let Garrett move twenty kilos of cocaine alone – so I agreed to help. Besides, once we'd complete this simple drop off, a quarter million was ours.

"You lucky you're my brother," I said leaning down to kiss Olivia. "I'll see you later baby. Keep that pussy wet for me."

She gave me a seductive smile and pushed me away. I grabbed the duffle bag hidden under my desk and walked out of my room.

Garrett grabbed the keys off the hook near the kitchen as we headed toward the door. A loud knocking came at our front door, stopping us in our tracks.

"You expecting somebody?' I asked.

"Hell no," Garrett said reaching for the gun in his back halter. He slowly walked forward and shouted, "Who is it?"

We listened for a few minutes but didn't hear anything. Before Garrett could ask again, shots rang through the front window.

"Fuck!" I yelled and dropped down to the ground.

"What the fuck?" Garrett yelled as he shot back at the window.

My heart pounded as a mixture of fear and anger washed over me. I knew we shouldn't have trusted that bitch ass homeboy of his. My breath caught as realization hit me.

"Shit, Olivia man!" I roared, feeling panic spread throughout my body.

"Make sure she's straight, I got you covered."

I nodded and ran to my room making sure to keep low. I didn't know who the fuck was shooting at us, but I swear if Olivia was hurt, I was going to kill all of them muthafuckas.

"Babe!" I shouted, hoping she could hear me over the loud gunshots.

"Here!" Olivia whimpered, her hand shooting up from underneath my bed. I reached for her and pulled her closer to me.

"Are you hurt?" she shook her head. "Stay close to me, I'll get you out of here."

I grabbed her hand and led her toward the backdoor. The fence around our house wasn't that high and I knew she'd be able to get over it. Suddenly, the room fell silent. My heart pounded against my chest as dread crept up my spine.

"Garrett?" I loudly whispered.

"I'm right here."

My shoulders dropped with relief but then Olivia dropped my hand and started walking toward the front door.

"What the fuck?" Garrett mouthed as I stared at her in confusion.

I watched as she stepped over Garrett and opened the front door. She looked over her shoulder and stared at me. I opened my mouth to call her, but she placed her fingers to her lips and winked. She let out a loud whistle and stepped aside. A few moments later, two tall and muscular men walked into our living room.

"Well?" a third man asked, but I couldn't see him from behind where I was crouching.

"It's right here," Olivia said holding up my duffle bag.

What the fuck? Shit, I must've dropped it during the shooting. The man closest to the door examined the contents of the product and nodded toward the leader before him as the other man hauled the bag out of the house.

"That's my girl," the mysterious man said. I could see his arm wrapped around her waist as he slapped her ass. Heat boiled throughout my body as the sound of their lips smacking together filled the room. I stared in disgust at Olivia's profile and started to move closer to get a view of the man she betrayed me with.

"You backstabbing bitch!" Garrett shouted, stopping me in my tracks. He rushed toward the door, but before I could stop him a loud bang echoed through my ears.

Smoke spilled from the gun and shimmered across the room. Time seemed to stand still as I watched in horror Garrett's body falling to the ground.

"Noooo!" I shouted and scrambled to my feet.

The sound of laughter hit me as the man walked away. I made a mental note that he had a knife tattoo on the side of his neck with a medium brown complexion.

I dropped down and scooped up Garrett in my arms. I clutched his head as blood filled his mouth. His pained eyes stared into me as he limply grabbed and squeezed my hand.

"Hold on man," I whimpered, trying to apply pressure to his chest. My vision began to blur as tears filled my eyes.

"Whom. Shall. I. Fear." Garrett rasped through breaths.

"Don't man! Don't preach to me right now when your God is trying to take you away from me. I'm not going to let that happen!"

A smirk spread across his face, and he slowly shook his head. "Get to know him. I want to see you in paradise one day."

"Don't leave me, man, please," I sobbed, staring down at him. A look of peace spread across his face as he squeezed my hand one last time and then his eyes went vacant.

"Sorry babe, but it's just business," Olivia said, hovering over me. She let out a vexed breath before leaning down and whispering in my ear, "I'm never going to find anybody that's going to fuck me the way you did. Oh well."

Nausea rolled through me as I glared up at her. She smirked at me before pointing at me. Shock began to fade as the end of the barrel pointing directly at me caught my attention. I held onto Garrett tighter as the gun shot off again.

***

I refilled my flask and took a long gulp of the whiskey I brought with me. I sat my head back against the bus seat and closed my eyes. I should've died that day with Garrett, but for some reason, I didn't. I couldn't understand why until now – it was to get my revenge.

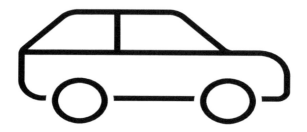

Chapter 11

Nicholas — Present

"What the fuck you mean I can't drink?" I shouted at the bus driver. "I paid my fucking ticket like everybody else on this bitch. Now do your job and drive. Stop worrying about what the fuck I'm doing."

We had just made it into Columbus when the acidity of alcohol and day-old burgers formed in my throat. The bathroom was preoccupied, and I had nowhere else to turn but to the empty seat next to me. The older woman behind me screamed so loud that the bus driver pulled off the road to investigate as I emptied my guts. It wasn't like I was trying to do it on purpose. Shit, if the couple in the bathroom wasn't fucking, the whole bus wouldn't be smelling like whiskey and vomit.

"Sir, per the terms and conditions listed on our website, alcoholic beverages are prohibited." The older pale man said, pointing his finger. The name tag on his uniform said Keith and I held back a laugh.

Why this scrawny old man named 'Keith' thought he was intimidating me was currently hysterical – or maybe it was the liquor making me feel amused.

"That's the stupidest shit I've ever heard," I said taking a swig from my flask. I instantly regretted it because I still had a bit of bile in my mouth. I bent over and spat it out on the ground. I would've felt bad, but there was already vomit there - oh, well.

"Ugh! Sir, throw out your flask or I am going to have to ask you to leave."

"Fuck you!" I spat wiping my mouth on the back of my hand.

"Exit the bus immediately, before I call the police," he demanded.

I smacked my lips and grabbed my duffle bag from under my seat. I stormed past the passengers glaring at me and jumped off the bus. The damn driver didn't even bother to close the door all the way before driving off. I looked around and saw a sign that read the nearest gas station was only half a mile away.

"Fuck it," I said, spitting on the ground as I began to walk. I figured I'd catch the next bus out, but I knew I'd have to wait a few hours. Oh, well, it'll give me some time to sober up and clean myself. I didn't want to be thrown off the next bus.

Forty-five minutes later I sludged through the parking lot. I would have made it a bit sooner, but all of the damn alcohol I had consumed over the past few hours decided to keep exiting my body. I smelled awful and needed to put some type of food in my stomach.

"Willy Earl?" a thick curvaceous woman shouted as she stepped out of her SUV.

She was fine as fuck with her thick brown hair in a messy bun and smooth tawny complexion that glistened when the sun hit. If she were trying to hide her shapely body, then her oversized long sleeve shirt wasn't doing its job. Her large breasts still poked out proudly while the shirt hugged her juicy ass. She had on a pair of black leggings that were almost see-through as she stood in the sun waving her hands in the air to flag down the tow truck. Her shirt slightly lifted, and I could see just a hint of her panty line against her luscious cheeks.

If I wasn't currently smelling like an old brewery and puke, I would've approached her. I licked my lips and stopped gawking at her. I could feel my dick waking up with excitement but now was not the time. Not that I wouldn't mind busting a quick nut before hitting the road again, but I needed to stay focused.

I readjusted my duffle bag on my back and headed toward the men's restroom. Thankfully, the gas station was also a popular rest stop for truck drivers and had showers available. I'd rather shower in a hotel, but beggars can't be choosers.

I turned on the water and waited for it to heat up. I gathered my soap, toothbrush, toothpaste, and a pair of sandals out of my bag. I didn't care how clean it looked; I was not about to place my bare feet on this floor. I undressed and threw my soiled clothes into the trash. It was only a plain back tee and a pair of sweatpants that I could replace. Besides, I didn't want to haul around dirty ass clothes.

My eyes closed as I stepped into the deliciously hot shower. I dipped my head back, letting the water soak my freeform locs and face. My thoughts flooded my head as I cleaned myself up. I wasn't happy with how I left home abruptly, but I've been looking for Olivia's ass ever since I woke up from the hospital.

She had shot me point blank, hitting me in the chest. When I woke up in the hospital, the doctor said that bullet the she placed in me had missed a major artery by less than a millimeter.

The police had no luck tracking her down over the past two years which, honestly, wasn't a surprise. We lived in a populated city aka the crime rate was through the roof.

I sighed as I lathered my body with soap. I should've been thankful to be alive, but I was pissed off. What still boiled my blood was the fact that she waited until I saw my brother's last breath before she decided to step in and shoot me. It was like she received full satisfaction watching me hold my brother as he died in my arms before she attempted to end my life – but that's where she fucked up. I was still alive. Thanks to Ayzo, though, her time was limited. I was coming after her ass, and nothing was going to stop me.

After I cleaned myself up and got dressed, I stepped out of the restroom feeling a lot better. I headed inside the store and bought myself two potato and egg breakfast burritos, some orange juice, and a bottle of water. I sat outside on the bench and searched for the next bus to Vegas.

"Alright now girly, I have the battery you asked for, but it looks like you're also a bit low on oil," the mechanic shouted from under the hood before facing her. He was a foot shorter than her and had a round pot belly that sat up high in his uniform – probably from a life of drinking beer. His black hair was thinning at the top of his head and his beard was not connected. He had dark chocolate wrinkled skin, and you could see his stained teeth as he puffed on the cigarette hanging from his ashen lips.

The woman I spotted earlier ran a hand over her face and slightly shook her head. "Unbelievable! My fiancé told me he got my oil changed out last weekend," she said, folding her arms.

"Well, er, I don't know what to tell you, but all I have to do is fill er' back up and you'll be good to go. Your drive to California should be smooth from there."

"That's good Mr. Willy Earl."

"Just call me Willy," he said drifting his eyes down her body.

"Oh, um thanks, Willy," she mumbled, shifting subtly away from him. "How much is this going to cost?"

"A job like this usually costs about five hundred."

I choked on the sip of orange juice I was taking. It was highway robbery for what that mechanic was charging that woman. He obviously was taking advantage of her dire situation and had no shame about it.

"Five hundred? For a battery and some oil?" the woman groaned. Her shoulders drooped as she dug into her purse to retrieve the money.

"You can pay when I'm done," the mechanic said licking his ashy lips.

She nodded and excused herself to the lady's room. Her head hung low as she walked past me, and I could've sworn I saw tears streaking from her adorable face. I shook my head in disgust toward the mechanic. I contemplated saying something, but honestly, it wasn't any of my business. I felt bad for the woman though.

The mechanic headed to his truck and pulled out the car battery she ordered and a small bottle of motor oil. He quickly replaced the battery and poured less than a tablespoon of oil into the engine. I shook my head and watched as he did a couple of tests to ensure her car started up. He stood in front of the woman's car with his hands on his hips and nodded - satisfaction blooming across his face.

"Five hundred dollars for a 15-minute job and so-called oil fill," I scoffed under my breath. The man must've heard me because he glared at me from the corner of his eyes.

"Damn kids ain't got no respect." He huffed out loud as he rolled his black eyes toward me.

He cleaned up his tools and placed them back into his truck before closing the hood of the woman's car. He eyeballed me up and down as he walked past. I blankly stared back at him as he headed toward the men's restroom. I scoffed and shrugged my shoulders focusing back on my phone - I was not intimidated by his old ass.

I found the next bus to Vegas leaving from Columbus, but the pickup point was an hour away by car. There was no way I'd make it in time by foot. I placed my head in my hands and let out a frustrated breath.

"Guess I'm getting a rental car," I grumbled out loud. I mindlessly thumbed through my missed notifications on the few social media sites I still had when I suddenly remembered I needed to look up Ayzo's friend Vincent's information.

It wasn't hard to find him as a buddy on Ayzo's friend list and the fool had his location turned on through the app. I didn't have his exact address, but he wasn't far from popular locations with addresses. All I would have to do is observe.

"Stop!"

I jolted my head away from my phone and looked around. My ears tingled as a muffled yelp came from the rest area followed by a door slamming. Adrenaline charging through me, I jumped up and headed toward the noise. As I got closer, I could hear the woman crying for help.

"Shut the hell up! All I am trying to do is give you another option to pay me," the mechanic sneered.

What the fuck? Her sobs became louder as another crash echoed from the men's bathroom. Without a second thought, I kicked down the door and was appalled at what I was seeing. The mechanic had the woman's arms pinned behind her back and her upper body leaning over the sink. He had the top half of his uniform off and was attempting to pull down her leggings.

I ran inside and wrapped my arm around his throat, putting him into a chokehold. He gasped for air and clawed at my arm.

"You sick son of a bitch!" I snarled in his ear as he fought against me.

I looked up at the woman who was trembling with fear. The mere thought of this nasty muthafucka putting his grimy hands on her enraged me. I let him go, but before he could take in air, I punched him square in the face. He instantly dropped to the ground and began coughing. Blood spilled down his nose as I towered over him. I reared my leg back and thrust my foot into his stomach. He yelled out a sharp cry as he doubled over in pain but that didn't stop me from repeatedly kicking him. Men like him were a fucking disgrace and I didn't give a fuck how bad I was hurting him.

"Sir," the woman whimpered causing me to stop mid-kick.

"Are you okay?" I asked still glaring down at him. My chest heaved with fury, and I wanted to stomp his head in until he was unconscious for even attempting to hurt her. Lord knows how many other unfortunate women that fell victim to him.

Realizing she hadn't answered, I snapped out of my trance and looked up at her. She was staring down at the man too. Her oversized shirt was still pulled up over her mid-drift and the right side of her leggings were pulled down exposing the top of her hip. Her tear-filled eyes met mine and she quickly nodded her head.

"C'mon, let's get out of here," I instructed, reaching out my hand.

She quickly grabbed onto me without taking her eyes off the mechanic. Her face was flushed, and her breathing was shallow as I guided her out of the bathroom and to the bench.

"I'll go get you some water," I said, attempting to walk into the store, but she tightened her grip on my arm.

"Please, don't leave me. I'm scared he'll come back," she said in a quiet shaky voice.

I highly doubted he'd be able to get up for a while after the beating I just gave him, but I nodded and sat next to her. After a few moments of sitting in silence, she let out a shaky breath and sniffled. She wiped away her tears with the back of her long-sleeved shirt and looked at me.

"Thank you for stepping in and helping me. He ambushed me outside of the lady's room and kept saying he had another option for me to pay. I realized what the hell was happening when he said Jean had found him a good one."

Lines formed in the middle of my eyebrows as I looked at her in confusion. "Who is Jean?"

"The woman I met earlier who called Willy Earl to help with my dead battery. I thought she was just an older woman trying to help me out...I guess not."

I shook my head in disgust. This is why I didn't trust anybody these days – everyone had evil intentions. Either they were after money, or they were after some type of power or control over another individual.

"I felt extremely uncomfortable and tried to call for help, but he covered my mouth and pushed me inside of the men's room," she said gripping the hem of her shirt and twisting it into her hand. "I made eye contact with a passing trucker, but he pretended like he couldn't hear me and walked off."

"Muthafucka!" I snarled balling my hands into fists. The primal need to protect her was pulsing in my veins.

"I'm okay," she said offering a small smile.

"Are you sure? Because I'll go beat his ass too!"

Her smile widened and a faint giggle escaped her lips. "I'm okay, really. I'm Ashlynn by the way."

"Nicholas," I said reaching out to shake her hand. She accepted it and I couldn't help but notice how soft she was.

"Nice to meet you, Nick."

I chuckled. She looked at me in confusion as she released my hand. "Sorry, it's just... nobodies called me Nick in a long time."

"Really? So, people just walked around saying Nic-ohl-as instead of just Nick?" she said stretching out my name and chuckling.

Her smile was contagious, and I found myself beaming at her. I shrugged my shoulders, "I guess so. Honestly, the last person to call me Nick was my brother."

My smile faltered with the thought of Garrett. It's funny, I hadn't been able to think of happier memories when he crossed my mind before. For the past two years, the only memory I had was of him dying in my arms.

"I'm sorry. I didn't mean to offend you or-," Ashlynn began to ramble.

"No, no it's cool. Nick is cool."

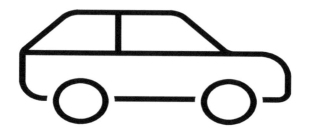

Chapter 12

Ashlynn

I found myself staring at Nick as he vacantly gazed out into the empty parking lot. I noticed how he got silent when he mentioned his brother and couldn't help but wonder what may have happened. I didn't want to pry into his business, though. So instead, sat in silence with him and stared up at the sky. I don't know why I didn't speak to him, but it just seemed like the right thing to do at the moment.

After a few moments, I glanced back at him from the corner of my eyes and couldn't help but notice how handsome he was. Not just by his looks either, but the fact that he didn't hesitate to step in and help me. My fucking hero. I bit my bottom lip as the thought of running my hands through his hair and wrapping my legs around his sturdy waist flashed through my mind.

Wait, no! I literally almost got assaulted not 10 minutes ago and here my dumb ass was fantasizing over this stranger. What the hell was wrong with me? Maybe I was still in shock, and I was only attracted by this strange man because he saved me. Yeah, that's it. I definitely did not want to climb him like a tree. Besides, I was engaged to be married – I couldn't do that to Bobby.

"Welp," Nick said, standing up. "I'm glad that you're okay now Ms. Ashlynn and I hope the rest of your travels are safe and uneventful. I have to get going if I am going to make it to the bus station."

I watched as he gathered his duffle bag. I chewed on my bottom lip and nervousness swam through my stomach. "Wait!" I said - well, more like yelled at him.

"Uh, yes?" he asked me with an arched eyebrow.

"I um- I was wondering if there was anything I could do to repay you? You saved me from a traumatic experience. I couldn't even imagine the things that would've happened to me if you hadn't shown up."

"It's no sweat. You don't owe me anything."

"How about I give you a ride?"

Hold up, what the hell did I just say? It's the twenty-first century, who the hell is still giving hitchhikers rides? Now I know I was definitely still in shock because ain't no way I just offered to have a complete stranger in my damn car. I've watched enough Dateline and listened to countless murder podcasts to know not to trust strangers. Especially ones hanging out at rest stops. Then again, if he wanted to hurt me, he would've joined that creepy ass mechanic in the bathroom or he would've just ignored me like the other guy.

He looked me over and scratched his thick black beard. "You don't know me from Adam, but you'll allow me to ride in the car with you?"

Taking a deep breath, I nodded. "I know we are complete strangers, but I oddly feel safe around you. I mean you've had plenty of chances to harm me or take advantage of me especially since I was just attacked, but you haven't."

He grunted before shoving his hands into his pockets. The bob in his throat moved up and down as he swallowed and stared at the ground.

"I get it. It's weird, but like I said, you saved my life and I want to repay you."

He rubbed the back of his neck and gazed at me with his warm hazel eyes. A look of concern etched across his face and his eyebrows furrowed. "I'm trying to get to Vegas." He finally said.

"That's on the way to California. I can drop you off on the strip, that way I can watch the water show at the Bellagio Hotel and play a few slots," I nervously laughed. I folded my arms and took a deep breath. "I oddly feel secure around you – hell you stepped in and beat somebody's ass for me. I'd feel better if you traveled with me."

A small chuckle escaped his lips as he readjusted his bag. "Fuck it, let's go."

A mixture of relief and anxiousness washed over me as we walked toward my SUV. I was worried about spending the next forty hours in the car with an absolute stranger, but it paled in comparison to being assaulted again. Especially if no one was available to help me and I couldn't fight off assailants on my own.

I grabbed my phone - thankful it was finally charged - and dialed Bobby to let him know what was going on. Disappointment swept over me when he sent my call to voicemail. It was only ten in the morning, and he was usually up. I left him a message to call me back as Nick placed his bag in the trunk of the car.

"Everything okay?" Nick asked as he sat in the passenger seat.

"Yeah," I said throwing my phone into the cup holder. "I was hoping to talk to my fiancé. I wanted to give him an update on everything that's been going on, but he didn't answer."

"Mmhmm," Nick said, nodding his head. "I'm sure he'll call you back."

I gave him a half smile before bowing my head and closing my eyes. I said a quick prayer thanking God for keeping me safe and sending Nick at the right time. I ended by asking for traveling graces and to give me a sign if I needed to kick Nick out of my car. I then glanced over and realized that Nick was staring at me.

"Is there a problem?" I asked, trying to keep the attitude from my voice. It never failed that someone had something to say when they saw me praying in public.

"What's your favorite Bible verse?"

"Huh…what?" I asked puzzled. I was 100 percent ready to defend my God, but Nick just threw me in for a loop.

"What's your favorite verse? I don't know too many of them yet since I'm a bit new in this Christian thing, but so far mine's 1st Corinthians 15 verse 58."

My cheeks flushed and I dropped my head in hopes of him not seeing the smile plastered on my face. It was something about a man who loved God that made my heart flutter. Bobby believed there was a higher power but didn't necessarily believe in God.

"Um, that's kind of tough – there's so many good ones," I cleared my throat and wiped my hands down my leggings. "It'll have to be between Psalms chapter 100 or 27."

Nick cringed and dug his fingers into his knees so hard I thought he was going to rip a hole into his pants. I held my breath as I watched him close his eyes and take a few shallow breaths. After a few moments of silence, Nick looked over at me and gave me a hesitant smile.

"I apologize Ashlynn. It's been a while since I heard anyone mention Psalms 27."

"Oh? Is there a certain reason why?"

"Yeah, but I'd rather not talk about it."

I gave him a tight lip smile and nodded as I started up the car. I must've hit another trigger for him. I made a mental note to not mention that verse or anything about his brother. In the meantime, I needed to rethink my conversational skills. I wasn't going to pressure him to talk but it would be nice to get to know the person I was going to spend the next three days with.

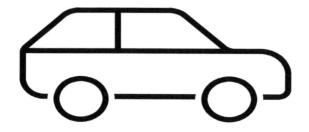

Chapter 13

Nicholas

Ashlynn drove for the next couple of hours allowing her collection of diverse music to shuffle on the Bluetooth radio. The car filled from 90s R&B to classic 80s rock music. A few popular boy bands from *NSYNC to Jodeci had her shamelessly singing her heart out. Hell, she even had me bobbing my head and humming when Rick James's Mary Jane came on.

"Do you smoke?" I asked as the song ended.

"Not anymore," she said, shaking her head. "I only like the song. Honestly, I only smoked before so that I could fit in at social gatherings. I never really understood the purpose of it."

"It's to get high," I said, shrugging my shoulders nonchalantly.

She laughed out loud, "Well, no shit Sherlock. I only meant that I personally didn't have a reason to smoke. It didn't really do anything for me. I mean no offense to you if you smoke."

"No, you good, I don't smoke."

"Do you drink?" she asked as Aerosmith's Dream On started to play.

I chewed my bottom lip and debated on what to tell her. I could easily say no, but for some reason, I didn't want to lie to her. I cleared my throat and stared down at my hands.

"Yes, I drink. A bit too much now lately to tell you the truth. I had a traumatic event happen two years ago, and it's been pretty hard to move on from it. Drinking has been my coping mechanism," I let out a disappointed chuckle. "Choosing some type of addiction seems to be the thing to do in my family instead of talking it out."

"I'm sorry you're going through that," she said in a sorrowful voice. "I know you don't know me, but I am here to listen if you want. I promise not to judge."

I nodded my head and swallowed the dry lump in my throat. The genuine sadness in her voice almost had me let down my guard. Outside of Ayzo, I lost trust in people, especially females. I refused to allow myself to be vulnerable again. From being betrayed by my mother when I was younger, to my ex-girlfriend, who could blame me?

Now a woman I barely knew was unknowingly ready to have me open up old wounds. I didn't understand how and why this was happening, but I needed to shut it down fast before I got hurt again. Ashlynn was nice, but still couldn't be trusted.

"So," I said clearing my throat, "Ms. Ashlynn, tell me about yourself. We're going to be together for the next 38 hours and I think we'll both feel better if we know a bit about each other."

"Well, I'm twenty-four, born in California but moved to Philadelphia when I was about eight.

"Oh shit, you live in Philly?"

"Yeah!" she nodded.

"Me too! I've been there my whole life – surprised I've never run into you before."

"I don't get out much. I mean I would every so often with my two homegirls, but I'm really a homebody. It's cheaper there."

I laughed, "You ain't never lied. Okay what else?"

"Hmm, let's see. Well, I went to the University of Pennsylvania and got my bachelor's degree in business management so I can eventually take over my dad's business. He's currently back in Cali looking for areas to expand."

I noticed how her grip tightened around the steering wheel. "Something tells me there's more than that," I said tapping my finger against the armrest.

She looked over at me briefly, before turning her attention back to the road. She waited a few moments before relaxing. "I guess it wouldn't hurt to tell you, I mean, it's not like we're going to be a part of each other's lives after this trip," she said, chuckling nervously.

"That's true," I agreed, giving her my full attention.

"Okay, well, I have no desire to take over my father's business."

"What type of business does he run?"

"He owns We Got Tires."

"Oh shit! Fo'real? I've been going there for years," I exclaimed. They were the only tire shop that I could trust. Plus, they always have good deals on rims.

She nodded proudly, "Yes indeed! My dad and my grandpa started the company from the ground up when we moved here. Don't get me wrong, I am happy for my family's success, it's just that —"

"You don't have the same passion as your dad for the shops," I said, finishing her sentence. She gave me a half grin and slowly nodded. "What is your passion then?"

She bit onto her bottom lip before looking at me with a smile. Her face glowed with excitement, and I felt my dick jump. She was already beautiful, but seeing her beaming was causing me to readjust in my seat so that she didn't see the fool attempting to wake up in my pants.

"I just completed all my classes to retrieve my cosmetology licenses — I took the test Saturday. I want to be like my dad when it comes to owning my own chain of shops, but I want them to be beauty salons, not automotive shops. I just haven't had the balls to tell him."

"So, is that why you're going to Cali? To finally tell him what you want?" I asked curiously.

"Yes and no," she murmured. She threw me a sideways glance as I stared, at her waiting for her to explain. "Yes, I will eventually build up the courage to talk face to face with my dad about my goals. Unfortunately, it's not why I am heading there at this moment. My grandpa's not doing so well, and we truly don't know if he'll even make it to the holidays. I wanted to see him before it was too late."

"Shit, I'm sorry to hear that."

"Thanks. It sucks because me and Grandpa have always been so close. He stuck by our side when my mom and grandma passed."

"Damn, you lost both of them at the same time?"

She nodded. "Car accident when I was seven. He was strong for both of us – even though he lost the love of his life. My dad took it hard, though. My mom was his everything and he pushed me and Grandpa away for a long time. Naturally, I reached out to my grandpa for everything. Even now, he's the first person I call, especially when my dad is being a dick," she sighed.

My eyebrows arched as I opened my mouth to ask her what she meant, but she held her hand up and shook her head.

"That's a long story that I really don't want to get into. So, what about you? What do you do or what are your goals? What's waiting for you in Vegas?" she asked.

"I'm meeting up with an old friend, but that's a long story that I really don't want to get into," I retorted.

"Touché," she nodded with a smirk.

"Right now, I don't really do much of anything besides volunteer at a few shelters or food pantries."

"You don't work?" she asked, wrinkling her brows.

"I technically don't need to, that's why I volunteer. Besides, I need to be able to come and go as I please to check up on my mom."

"You and your mom must be close."

"Nope," I said nonchalantly.

She looked at me from the corner of her eyes as she merged lanes on the highway, but I just stared ahead. I was in no mood to talk to her about me and my mom's relationship.

"Uh, okay. What about your goals?"

"Well, I was talking to my brother a few years ago about investing my money into a few businesses and maybe traveling."

"Wow! You rolling in money like that?"

I rolled my eyes and folded my arms across my chest. It didn't surprise me that she was getting excited about what could possibly be in my bank account. All these damn females were the fucking same.

"So, what do you like to do?" I asked, changing the subject. I didn't want to say something foul and get kicked out of the car. Besides, why should I get upset about what I already knew would happen? Women naturally were attracted to men with money.

"I like to watch movies, read, and hang out with my homegirls."

"What do you like to read?"

Her cheeks flushed as embarrassment took over. "I uh- I like steamy romance."

I smiled, "Ah, I see. No judgment here – I've read a few smutty books." She glanced over at me, and I gave her a playful wink. She laughed as relief washed over her.

"So, he reads?"

"Indeed, but I'm more of a mystery or suspense type of guy. So, you mentioned you liked movies."

"That's right."

"Let me ask you this, which Friday was better? The first, second, or third?"

"Even though the first one is a classic and Money Mike was freaking hilarious in the third one, the second one is my favorite."

"What? Really?"

"Hell yes! Pinky and Day-Day had me rolling. 'Say another. Mother fuckin word. And this shit is over. I ain't playin' nigga!'" she said, quoting one of Pinky's lines in the movie.

We both laughed out loud. Heat coursed through my body as I watched her face light up with amusement. The sweet sound of her laughter had my dumb ass dick jumping again and ready to bury deep in between her thick thighs. I wondered what her moans would sound like in my ear as I dug deep inside her. I shook my head. I didn't want to think like that with her. Yes, she was fine and thick, but I wasn't interested in bedding her. Well, that's what I kept trying to tell myself.

I readjusted in my seat, "Okay, name your top five favorite black and non-black movies," I instructed leaning back in my seat.

"Hmm," she thought for a few minutes. "Okay in no particular order, my top black movies are Juice, The Wood, The Five Heartbeats, Kingdom Come, and Coming to America. My top non-black movies are The Shawshank Redemption, The Breakfast Club, Misery, Bad Words, and Bullet Train."

"Damn, you like a lot of the same movies I do. I would swap out Coming to America for Menace to Society and Kingdom Come with Boyz in the Hood though."

"I should've known you were going to mention those two movies."

"I mean, they are classics," I said shrugging.

"Yeah, yeah. Okay, what are your non-black movies?"

"Easy - Liar Liar, The Mask, Pulp Fiction, Bad Lieutenant, and Kill Bill, preferably volume two."

Ashlynn smiled and glanced over at me again.

"What?" I asked.

"Nothing. It's just I haven't been able to laugh and talk about movies in a while."

"You and your fiancé don't talk about movies?" I asked, nodding toward the wedding band on her finger. I thought it was strange that she only had a basic band instead of an engagement ring especially since wedding bands only came after the marriage, but it wasn't my business.

She gripped the steering wheel and shook her head. "I mean, we kind of talked when we first got together, but it was Bobby who was doing most of the talking. I know what he likes and dislikes, but I'm not so sure if he remembers mine."

"So, you have been with him for how long now, and he doesn't know that one of your favorite movies is Juice?" I asked, sitting up in my seat.

"He's- he's busy. He has to manage five of my dad's shops and just has a lot on his plate. What does it matter that he doesn't know what my favorite movie, book, or food is." She said, irritably.

"He's too busy to remember the little things? I don't know Ashlynn, it's none of my business, but why would you want to marry somebody who doesn't have time for you?"

She glared at me from the corner of her eyes as her jaw clenched. "You're right, it isn't any of your business."

I nodded. It would be a wise choice to keep my mouth shut for a little while, so I didn't get kicked out of her car. Besides, she was right, it wasn't my business. Why should I care about her relationship, anyway? We weren't friends, but travel associates. I had no interest in her drama – I had enough of that on my plate. I was on a mission, and I wasn't about to get distracted from it.

I stared out the window adoring the sun-bathed open road as we passed through Ohio. The different hues of fall decorated the tress across the landscape creating a serene and breathtaking view. I hadn't been outside of Philly in years, and I forgot how beautiful the rest of the world was.

"I'm pulling into the gas station to use the restroom," Ashlynn mumbled. I looked over at her as she chewed her lip and drummed her fingers idly against the steering wheel. I wished Garrett was here right now. He knew how to de-escalate an uncomfortable situation.

A few moments later, we pulled into the parking lot. She hopped out of the car and rushed inside towards the restroom. I got out of the car and stretched. I didn't want to leave the car unlocked so

I decided to wait until Ashlynn returned. My stomach rumbled and the delicious smell of pizza filled the air.

"Are you hungry?" I asked as Ashlynn came out of the store.

"Uh, no I'm okay."

I cocked my head to the side and observed her as she wrapped her arms around her stomach. "When was the last time you ate?"

"Yesterday afternoon," she whispered.

"And you're not hungry?"

"Why, because I'm fat?" she snapped at me.

"What? No! Because it's been over 24 hours, and you haven't eaten." I said, with an arched brow.

She looked up at me and shook her head. "I'm just not hungry. I'm trying to lose weight so I can fit into my wedding dress."

I scratched my beard and stared at her. Her honey brown eyes glazed back at me with a pleading look to not ask any more questions. As much as I wanted to pry, I didn't and clamped my mouth shut. Maybe she was used to not eating for long periods of time, but I wasn't.

I headed inside the store and grabbed a few bags of chips, bottles of water, a sharable size bag of peanut M&Ms, and a few slices of pepperoni pizza from the bakery section. I headed back to the car and fumbled through the bag, eager to shove the delectable food in my mouth.

"How about I take over driving for a bit so you can rest?" I asked taking a bite of my pizza. Skepticism etched across her face as she considered my offer. I finished my slices and threw away my trash before she finally agreed and handed me the keys.

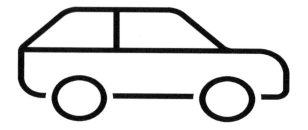

Chapter 14

Ashlynn

I wanted a bite of that fucking pizza, but I be damned if he stared at me judgmentally as I ate. I honestly shouldn't give a rat's ass, but I was insecure. The last thing I wanted was to have this unmistakably fine ass stranger look at me with disgust as I ate. Hell, I even caught Bobby looking at me with revulsion when food was involved sometimes. I would rather starve than see that look cross anyone's face.

"I'm going to fill up the tank," Nick said. I reached for my purse, but he shook his head and pulled out his wallet. He grabbed a credit card, threw his wallet back onto the driver's seat, and closed the door.

I licked my lips as I watched him walk away. That man was absolutely delicious, and I had no business lusting for him. I couldn't help it though, especially when I realized he had a small stud in his nose and his ears were pierced. I was so traumatized with the attack earlier, that I didn't notice. Now that I've had the time to actually observe him, it was becoming hard to not get my panties wet. Piercings on a man was a major turn on for me. I've tried a few times to suggest Bobby get his ears pierced, but he refused.

"Nope! I cannot think like that," I said out loud reaching down to grab my phone and purse. Two more hours had passed since I last tried calling Bobby and I thought he should for sure be up by now.

As I dialed Bobby's number, I took forty dollars out of my purse. I shoved it in Nick's wallet when I saw a picture jammed in between his cards. I checked around to see if Nick had made it back before examining the picture. He was resting his chin on top of a petite Latina woman as he embraced her from behind. They looked genuinely happy with their matching black hoodies, blue jeans, and all white Nikes.

A hint of jealousy etched up my spine as I stared at the woman. She was utterly beautiful with her long brown hair and small Coke bottle frame that Nick proudly held onto. I shook my head and placed the picture back into his wallet. Why did I need to be envious of Nick and his girlfriend when I had Bobby?

I refocused on my phone and continued to listen as the phone rang. I was just about to hang up when an out of breath Bobby answered the phone.

"H-hey Lynn!" he said in a breathy voice.

"Hey! I've been trying to reach you for hours. Is everything okay?" I asked.

"Huh? Oh, yeah everything's cool over here. Sorry, I must've had my phone on silent earlier."

"What are you doing? You sound out of breath."

"I just got done playing a pickup game at the rec center. You know I like to play at least one basketball game on Sundays."

"Oh right! Sorry I didn't mean to interrupt, but a lot has happened since I been on the road." I said, running my hand down the side of my face.

"Where are you now? " Bobby hurriedly asked.

"I'm not sure, maybe just outside of Dayton. I remember seeing a sign saying I was a few hundred miles from either Chicago or Indianapolis. I was just about to fill up on gas and maybe grab a bite to eat."

"Didn't you pack some protein bars with you?"

"Uh, no. Why?" I asked hesitantly. I felt the knot forming in the pit of my stomach because I knew where this conversation was going.

"Just asking. I would hate for you to gain weight while you were on the road because you were eating only fast food like you usually do when you're nervous or stressed. Try to get you a salad or a veggie wrap somewhere if you can't get a protein bar."

And there it was. Tears brimmed at the edge of my eyes as I held the phone in silence. I was really trying hard to lose weight, but that didn't matter to Bobby. In his eyes, I was running to food every time a minor incident occurred in my life.

"Look, I got to go they want me to play another game."

"But- "I protested but was interrupted by a beeping noise indicating the call ended.

No longer having the strength, I let the tears roll down my face. I could not wrap my head around what I was doing wrong. Maybe I was putting too much pressure on him and that's why he was pushing away from me. I mean I am constantly begging him for sex or for us to spend time together when I know he works ten to twelve hours a day, five to six days a week. I wish he would just talk to me and tell me what I was doing wrong so that I could fix it.

I quickly wiped my face as I saw Nick heading back to the car. He had more snacks with him as he waved a bottle of Gatorade and a black bag at me. He opened the door while sitting the bag on the seat.

"I know you said you weren't hungry, but I got you a slice of pizza and you have to at least stay hydrated, hence the Gatorade. I hope you like the red-" Nick said fumbling through the bag. He stopped mid-sentence when he finally looked up at me. The proud look he had on his face vanished. "What's wrong?"

I put on the best smile I could muster up and shook my head. I didn't want to open my mouth to speak because I knew the waterworks would start all over again. His eyes stared at my hands gripping my phone. He opened his mouth to say something but quickly closed it again. He handed me the drink and pizza slice before he turned to pump the gas.

I took a few sips and stared down at the pizza box. I quickly ate the slice keeping an eye on Nick to ensure he didn't see me. I gulped down more of the Gatorade before laying back on the headrest. That was delicious, but I couldn't eat that much junk. The car shifted under Nick as he slid into the driver's seat and closed the door.

He didn't bother to look over at me which was fine. I was embarrassed and wasn't up for more talking. Instead, I closed my eyes and let sleep wash over me.

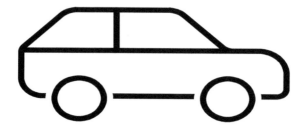

Chapter 15

Nicholas

I had no idea what happened from the time I went into the store to the time I made it back to the car, but I was lowkey pissed. Ashlynn and I may have started off rocky, but I didn't think it was that bad. Then again, I had been prying into her business. Shit.

I wanted to make things right so that I could see the adorable way she blushed when she was nervous or how she chewed on her bottom lip when she wanted to say something but was too afraid. Oh, and don't get me started on her smile. She was so beautiful when she smiled that it could brighten up anyone's day.

Even though I was never going to show my vulnerability and let my guard down around another woman, something about Ashlynn was different. I still didn't know if I could fully trust her, but a small voice in the back of my mind was telling me that I could. She seemed like a genuine person.

So, when I got back to the car and saw that she had clearly been crying, I wanted to kick myself. I made her feel bad about her fiancé even though I knew nothing about him. From the little that she told me, the man seemed like a straight up jackass, but I had no right to judging their relationship.

I looked over at her as she quietly slept, and I wanted to do nothing more than pull the car over to hold her in my arms. Her stomach gurgled and she winced in pain as she wrapped her arms around her waist. Was she starving herself? I mean she mentioned she had to lose some weight to get into her wedding dress – personally, I thought she was gorgeous the way she was.

I slowed at a four-way stop sign that led me back to the highway when I noticed her phone had lit up with a text notification. I didn't want to pry, but hey, curiosity killed the cat. I previewed the message so it would still show up as unread.

Bobby: *Hey Lynn, I read that smoothies are good meal replacements instead of eating all of that fattening junk that you'd normally get. You'll be in a size twelve in no time! I can see your fine self in your wedding gown now looking scrumptious and thin! I'll call you in a few hours, Love yah.*

My jaw hung low as I stared at the phone. Was this muthafucka serious? Who the hell gaslights their significant other about their weight? I placed the phone back and huffed out air. I see now why she was crying.

A honk came from behind me. I poked my head out of the window to see a white car waiting for me to go. I pushed the hazard lights on and motioned my arm for them to go around me. No one else was at the stop sign and I should have left a while ago, but I couldn't. I didn't want Ashlynn to wake up and cry some more after reading that fucked up message.

I didn't know what to do so I grabbed my phone and dialed Ayzo's number. I kept the hazard lights on as I stepped out of the car and leaned against the door.

"Well, well, well," Ayzo said answering his phone. "If it isn't Mr. Leave My Friend At The Bar To Seek Out a Pointless Revenge Avery. How you doing, sir?"

"Ayzo, c'mon man, I didn't call to argue."

"Are you still headed to Vegas?"

"Hell yeah. I told you Olivia has to pay for her sins!" I barked at him. Ayzo let out a groan.

"I love you brother and I hope that you remember what the good book says about revenge. On that note, I'll just agree to disagree with you. So, what's up?"

I proceeded to tell him everything that's happened from the time I stormed out of the bar to standing now against the car. I told him about the messed-up text message from Ashlynn's fiancé and how I felt bad for her.

"Damn Nicholas, how have you been able to go through so much shit in the past twenty hours?"

"Who knows bro? What do you think I should do about Ashlynn? I mean, I don't want her to be sad when she wakes up."

"Yeah, that was a messed-up text. And she's supposed to be marrying that clown?" Ayzo scoffed. "Where you at now?"

"Uh, I can't see my GPS, but I remember passing a sign that said we were a few hundred miles from Chicago and - "

"Bro, take her to the Navy Pier," Ayzo interrupted excitedly. "Unless you have her passcode, it's inevitable that she'll see that text. So, to lessen the blow, take her to play a few games or get on a few rides. Personally, I loved just walking through the area and enjoying the view."

"That's a good idea – it'll extend our trip some, but at least we'll be able to enjoy ourselves. I'll make sure to get us a hotel there too so we can get some rest afterward."

"Mmmhmm, a hotel huh?" Ayzo joked.

"Not like that fool. We're going to have two separate rooms. I'm not about to spit game at her."

"Why? Is she face-challenged?"

"Hell no. She's actually beautiful as fuck and it's kind of hard to keep my mind focused."

"So, what's the problem? I know it's not because she's engaged – that shit hasn't stopped you before."

"I know, but…Man, I don't know. I just can't bring myself to hurt her like that. She's genuinely nice and pleasant to be around. Oh, and bro she is hilarious. She did this spot-on Pinky impression earlier that had me dying laughing." I smiled, trying to hold back a laugh.

"I never thought I'd see the day," Ayzo said in a cheerful, satisfied voice.

"What?" I asked, arching my eyebrows.

"Nicholas Avery is infatuated with a woman again - that didn't have to involve sex."

"Chill out bro – it's not even like that," I said, rubbing the back of my neck and fighting the smile that wanted to invade my lips. "Ashlynn is cool people."

"Call it what you want Usher, but you got it bad," Ayzo said, and proceeded to sing the song.

"Alright bro, I'll call you later," I said and hung up the phone. I shook my head with laughter as I typed in the address to the Navy Pier.

Ayzo was a trip. As soon as I showed a tiny bit of interest in the opposite sex and it wasn't because I was trying to get in between their legs, Ayzo thought I was in love. I mean sure, he was right about my feelings for Olivia when I started to hang out with her. And ever since then, he thought he was a damn love guru. This time, he was definitely wrong. Ashlynn was getting married and besides once she dropped me off in Vegas, I highly doubted I'd ever see her again.

An ache began to throb in my chest as I merged onto the highway. The thought of not seeing her after this road trip made my stomach drop.

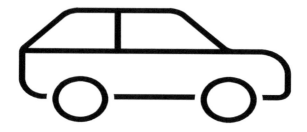

Chapter 16

Ashlynn

I slowly opened my eyes to the brilliant view of a sunset spread across the open sky. I looked over at Nick and blinked a few times. He was singing along to Giveon's Heartbreak Anniversary…stunningly. His deep voice was smooth and velvety – I was instantly hypnotized by his melodious tune.

"You sound amazing Nick," I said in a trance, feeling heat creep in between my legs.

He slowed at a stop light and looked over at me. A small grin crept at the corner of his mouth as he quickly looked away with embarrassment.

"Sorry, I didn't mean to wake you."

"No, I was just waking up when I heard you. Nick, you have an amazing voice! Have you ever thought of pursuing music?"

"Thanks," Nick said with a nervous chuckle. "I only sing for fun. I don't want to turn it into a chore. Plus, I haven't let anyone hear me sing in a long time."

"Your girlfriend doesn't get to hear your incredible voice?" I asked, sitting up in my seat and stretching.

The muscles in his jaws ticked as he gripped the steering wheel.

"I don't have a girlfriend," he grunted.

"I'm sorry, I just assumed – I mean you looked so happy in the picture in your wallet-,"

"You went through my wallet?" Nick asked, looking over at me.

"No! I mean kind of," I stammered out. "I'm sorry. I was just paying you back for the gas when I saw the picture sticking out. I swear, I didn't go Dora on your wallet."

"Go Dora?" he repeated in confusion.

"Yeah. I didn't go exploring in your belongings."

He stared at me for a brief moment before bursting out into laughter. "Ashlynn," he gasped, trying to catch his breath. He wiped away tears that had formed at the corner of his eyes from him laughing so hard and took a few breaths. "Girl, you are goofy! I ain't never heard no shit like that. I'ma have to use that – going Dora in some shit."

I chuckled with him and folded my arms across my lap. "I try to warn people ahead of time that I can be quite random and goofy."

"No sweat Lynn, I like that. It feels good to laugh," Nick said, staring at me. He shook his head, "Anyway it's no biggie - about the wallet thing. I've been meaning to burn that damn picture anyway. I do have a confession though. I sort of read a text message from your phone earlier."

He looked over at me with dreadful eyes as he pulled into a crowded parking lot.

"You read one of my text messages?" I asked, taking in my surroundings.

"Yes, I'm sorry I should have never invaded your privacy like that. It's just I saw your fiancé had texted you and was going to wake you up since I knew you've been waiting on him."

I arched a brow and looked over at my phone which was on the charger face down. Nick gazed at me and flicked his tongue across his bottom lip. I reached for my phone when he gently placed his hand over mine.

"What?" I asked in a nervous tone.

"I uh," a mixture of agony and fury flashed across his face before he moved his hand. He gave me a tight-lipped grin and stepped out of the car.

Full of anxiety, I snatched up my phone. My heart dropped and a lump swelled in my throat. Bobby's words cut me deep, but it wasn't anything new. Hell, I was expecting for him to text me sooner or later as soon as I mentioned food. He never missed an opportunity to tell me about the latest diet trend or to remind me how my eating habits could be altered.

I was frankly more humiliated that Nick read this message. I shouldn't care but for him to see how my fiancé talked to me, made me feel small and weak. A light tap came from my window as Nick stood before me. I swallowed the lump in my throat and counted to five before opening the door.

"I hope you don't mind, but I wanted us to have a little fun tonight."

My eyebrows shot up as heat flushed my face. "Have fun?"

"Yeah! No - not like that, but I mean maybe for the night we could be kids again. I know you have a lot going on and so do I. My homeboy said this was a great place to unwind and we could start fresh tomorrow. I'll pay for everything, so you don't have to worry."

I couldn't stop the smile from forming. Nick was really trying to make me feel better after reading the bullshit ass text I received. This man hardly knew me and had already done so much for me. He came to my rescue when that old pervert tried to assault me in the bathroom and now, he was coming to my rescue from my fiancé. Bobby had no problem with being blunt with me, but never took the time to make it right with me. Nick only read a snippet of what Bobby said to me and was going out of his way to make me feel better.

"Well?" Nick asked, extending out his arm.

I happily accepted it. "I've never been on a Ferris wheel."

"Well Lynn tonight we are going to ride every ride and eat until we burst." Nick proclaimed, guiding us to the entrance.

"I still have to fit into a wedding dress," I halfheartedly laughed.

He stopped in his tracks and pulled me closer to him. He dipped his chin and pierced his hazel eyes into mine. "You are beautiful just the way you are. Who gives a fuck about some size twelve dress, Ashlynn. It shouldn't matter if you had on a one-of-a-kind gown or a trash bag, your fiancé should love you regardless. If you want to lose weight, then cool, as long as you are happy and you're doing it for you. For anybody who says differently, they can kiss that juicy ass of yours - no offense."

Butterflies fluttered in my core as Nick observed me. His eyes darted to both of mine before trailing down to my lips. He slowly licked his own before refocusing his gaze back to my eyes. Maybe it was the cool fall air, but a shudder ran up my spine. I shifted my weight on my other foot and felt the dampness in between my legs. Okay, it definitely wasn't the brisk air that was making me shiver.

"Thank you," I said in a breathy voice. "For um, for being so nice to me."

Nick blinked and a smirk grazed his lips as he winked at me. He tightened his grip slightly around my arm as he led me to the ticket booth.

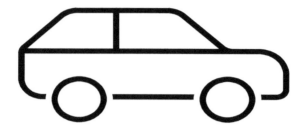

Chapter 17

Nicholas

Watching Ashlynn explore the wharf made me feel something I hadn't in a long time. What was this woman doing to me? Maybe it was the way she grinned after she'd won the biggest prize at the ring toss booth. Or the way her eyes lit up when she saw the ball hit the bell at the top of the tower during the Hi-Striker's game. She thought I wasn't paying attention to the way she ravenously stared at me when I slammed the mallet down against the base. We got on the last ride, the Ferris Wheel.

"I have a secret," she said, playfully bumping against me.

"What's that?"

"I am terrified of heights," she said taking in a slow breath, "But it is beautiful out here." She observed the dark pier as her hands gripped the bar in front of us. We were stopped at the top of the Ferris wheel looking down at the mixture of festive lights from each ride and swarms of pedestrians.

She tilted her head back and pointed at a cluster of stars. "There's the big dipper!"

"Damn for real?" I asked, leaning forward and following where she was pointing.

"Hell if I know," she said and looked at me from the corner of her eyes.

"Girl, you a trip," I said laughing and leaned back in my seat.

"I'm glad you laugh at my corny jokes. Bobby gets annoyed most of the time." Ashlynn said leaning back next to me. The excited look she had on her face staggered to a grimace.

"Can I ask you a question?"

"Only if I get to ask you one," she retorted.

"Alright, that's fair. You first."

"What happened to you and the woman in that picture in your wallet."

My nostrils flared as I stared out into the dark water. "She, uh...she betrayed me in the worst possible way imaginable. She pretended to care about me but in the end, it was all an act to get her hands on to a lot of money."

Pain dilated her eyes. "I'm...I'm sorry Nick. That's terrible. What did she do?"

I shook my head and kept my face blank as my eyes followed the waves beneath me. I wasn't going to tell her everything about that day. Why should I? I mean if I did, she'd see how exposed I was and on the verge of a mental breakdown. I had to admit though, it felt nice talking to her.

Damn, I missed Garrett.

I felt Ashlynn inch closer to me. After a few seconds, she placed her hand on the middle of my back, causing me to flinch. She stilled but did not remove her hand. Instead, she slowly began to rub my back in small gentle circles.

I closed my eyes as I unintentionally leaned into her touch. It had been so long since anyone comforted me. Ever since my mom shoved us into the arms of a drug dealer, all affection went out the window. Hell, even Olivia didn't allow me to show any type of weakness around her. She used to say only bitches showed their emotions.

"Nick, I can't begin to imagine the shit that you've been through, but I know one thing. You are strong and blessed."

I peeked over at her and let her heartwarming grin ease my nerves. I smiled back and ran my hand down my face. "Okay, my turn."

"Shoot," she said, dropping her hand from my back. I instantly missed her touch.

"Why do you let your fiancé belittle you like that?"

She chewed on her lip as she shifted uneasily in her seat. "I-uh I don't know to be honest with you. He never used to do that. Before we got engaged, Bobby was compassionate, caring, and romantic. We used to find a different restaurant every weekend to explore and spent the whole night flirting.

"Ever since my dad made him the general manager of his shops, he's been super stressed out. Don't get me wrong, he loves his job and isn't afraid to work, it just causes a strain on our relationship sometimes. I mean I understand that when he lashes out at me, I shouldn't take it personally."

"I guess," I said, rubbing my chin.

"What do you mean, you guess?" Ashlynn asked, folding her arms.

"Nothing, nothing."

"Don't do that Nick! Spit it out."

I sighed and turned to face her, "I don't care how much I had to work or how stressed I was at a job; I wouldn't dare talk to my woman the way that he talks to you. If you were my girl, I'd spend every chance I had telling you how amazing you are."

Tears began to well in her eyes and I immediately regretted it. Why the hell did I tell her all of that? I was supposed to be here making her feel better, but here I was making shit worse.

"Shit, I'm sorry Lynn," I said pulling her into my arms.

She shook her head as she rested on my chest. "No, it's not that Nick. You're right. I think me and Bobby had been together for so long, that I just accepted whatever he said to me. I've been so entranced with the thought of being married that I didn't stop to think if he was the one I wanted to spend the rest of my life with."

I cupped my finger under her chin and tilted her head back to meet my eyes. "You don't have to settle for anyone or anything that doesn't make you happy."

We gazed into each other's eyes, and I could feel her body tremble underneath me. We moved so close to each other that it seemed we were sharing the same air. I wanted to feel her luscious lips on mine and gotdamn, she felt so good in my arms.

The Ferris wheel creaked snapping us out of our trance as we began to descend back to the ground. Ashlynn cleared her throat and gently pushed away from me as she sat back on her side of the seat. I straightened and rubbed the back of my neck. We didn't say anything else the rest of the way down.

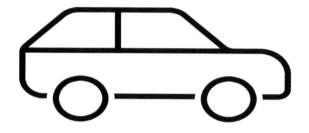

Chapter 18

Ashlynn

I almost made a terrible mistake. What the hell was I thinking, about to kiss Nick like that? I mean sure, I wanted to taste his lickable lips and run my hands across his strong body, but I was not about to betray Bobby like that.

Who was I kidding? Bobby has been treating me like crap and making me feel disgusted in my own body. He was allowing the stress from work to enter our home and it was putting a strain on our relationship.

Then again, I still loved him. How could I just throw away two and a half years down the drain without trying to attempt to fix the problem? All we needed was to complete some pre-marital counseling so that we could find better ways to openly talk to one another. Bobby could learn how to delegate so that we could spend more time together. While I could learn to not be so offended every time my future husband reminded me of my goal to lose weight.

"So, I got us a room at the Hilton a few blocks away," Nick said, after we reached my car. "Separate rooms of course."

"Thanks. How much do I owe you?"

"Don't worry about it," he said, climbing into the driver's seat.

Before I could complain, my phone rang. Bobby's name flashed across my screen. Nick looked at the phone and back at me before pulling out of the parking lot.

"Hey, Bobby."

"Hey Lynn, sorry it took me so long to call you back. You know how I get when I'm at the rec center."

"Yeah," I fake chuckled.

"Look, baby, I just wanted to apologize for what I texted you earlier. I don't know why I sent that stupid shit. It's just that I've been so worried about this inspection tomorrow at work that I took it out on you. It's honestly why I stayed at the center all day – wanted to clear my head."

"You really hurt my feelings," I groaned.

"I know and you did not deserve that. How can I make it up to you?"

"Stop being a dick," Nick mumbled under his breath.

"What was that?" Bobby asked.

I shot Nick a dirty look and turned down the volume on my phone. "It was nothing love. I was saying I forgive you. I know how much is on your plate right now. Just stay positive and don't worry, you'll get the store passed for the inspection."

"Thanks, baby you are too good to me," Bobby cooed.

I caught a glimpse of Nick rolling his eyes.

"You know I'd do anything for you love." I said, turning to face the window. We just pulled into the parking lot of the hotel. Nick hopped out of the car and slammed the door behind him.

What the hell was his problem?

"Have you talked to your dad today?" Bobby asked, breaking my glare from the back of Nick's head.

"No, why?"

"Well, he was thinking about retiring early so that he could spend more time with your granddad. It sounded as if he wanted us to officially take over the stores."

"Wh-what?" I stammered.

"Yeah! Isn't that great news? We could run the stores together, it'd be fun. I mean I'd handle all of the day-to-day business while you handle the books and accounting."

He had to be joking. Even if I wanted to help run the stores, why the hell did Bobby think I wanted to sit in the back office and only handle the accounting portion? Hell, I might as well stay at my current damn job.

"Bobby, I just made it to my hotel. Let me shower and get settled in then I can call you back." I expressed as Nick walked back to the car.

"No!" Bobby blurted. "I mean, no baby it's getting late. How about you get some rest and just text me in the morning? I can call you tomorrow after the inspection to let you know how it goes."

"Oh. Okay. Well, goodnight and I love you."

"Night. Love you too babe."

Nick handed me my room key and told me I was on the third floor without bothering to look up at me. I nodded and got out of the car. Ever since Bobby called, his mood had changed. We were literally having so much fun at the pier and got close – a bit too close – but close, nonetheless. Now he was cold and stand-offish. Hell, he wouldn't even look at me. Oh, well. Why should I care anyway? I was only going to be stuck with him for three more days then he'd be out of my life. A small ache formed in my chest with that thought.

I quickly snatched up my suitcase as Nick approached and grabbed his duffle bag. We walked inside the hotel still not uttering a word to each other. We stepped onto the elevator and waited to reach our floor. The air was thick with tension, and I found myself taking deep breaths to calm my racing heart.

"I'm sorry about the Ferris wheel," I blurted out. "I was caught up in my emotions and it felt good to be held at the time and I…," my voice trailed off as Nick looked down towards me causing me to clamp my mouth closed. He was already taller than me, but the way his eyes bore into me made me feel like a small child.

The elevator stopped and the doors opened onto the third floor. I scurried out and searched for my room door. The exasperated look of pain and annoyance from Nick had me remembering that he was still a complete stranger. I had only known him for the day and had no idea what was going on in his head. He didn't seem like he'd hurt me, but I still needed to stay cautious.

I reached my door and swiped the key letting myself into a queen-sized hotel suite. As I turned to bolt the door shut, Nick was opening his door directly across the hall. He looked over his shoulder and eyeballed me up and down. A small smirk formed on his lips before he went inside and bolted the door close. I let out a breath I didn't know I was holding before closing myself inside the room.

After I showered and stuffed myself with a chicken Caesar salad, I was ready to call it a night. It was just after 11 p.m. and I wanted us to be on the road no later than nine. I figured Nick was already asleep because it was completely quiet in his room when I left to pick up my food.

I turned off the TV and snuggled in bed. My mind wandered to the way Nick's eyes hungrily gazed at me and how he was mere inches from kissing me with those full luscious lips of his. I let my hand slowly drift down my nightgown and imagined it was Nick's. The way his strong arms wrapped around me had me slipping my fingers into my panties. It was true I still had no idea who he was, but instead of frightening me, it turned me own more.

Just as I closed my eyes and prepared to dive a finger into my opening, a clumsy thud followed by giggling was outside of my door. I rolled my eyes and chalked it up to some teenagers playing around in the hallways. Before I could refocus on reaching the sweet spot that'll send me into an orgasmic coma, a knock came at my door. I lifted my head and glared into the dark room. I waited a few moments before the knock came at my door again. I jumped out of bed and cursed under my breath.

"I swear if some badass kids are playing on people's doors, I'm going to shove my foot up somebody's ass," I grumbled tying the complimentary robe around my body.

I looked through the peephole but did not see anyone in the hall. I turned to get back in bed when the rapping at the door continued.

"Ugh!" I groaned. I threw the chain off of the hook and snatched the door open. The anger I was ready to implode on the intruder diminished as Nick stood before me. Shirtless.

"Did you eat," he slurred leaning against the doorframe.

I couldn't help but stare at his sturdy frame. His chest was bare except for a tattoo on his left upper pectoral. The illustration of a pair of wings surrounded a deformed circular scar. My eyes widen with the realization that it was a bullet wound. Who the hell shot him? I swallowed as I took a step back from the door.

"Uh- don't you think it's a bit too late to be thinking about food?" I asked arching an eyebrow. I sniffed and frowned. The lingering odor of alcohol filled my nose.

"Depends on the food you want to eat," he said licking his lips. His glazed over eyes trailed down from my face to my thighs. There was no mistaking the heat that clouded his gaze as he took a step closer to me, eliminating the space I placed in between us.

"Nick, I think you need to go lay down," I said, tightening my hold on the door.

"Ashlynn," Nick rasped my name, taking another step closer. "The things I would do to you if you just gave me the word."

The heat from his breath brushed against my lips, causing a shudder to run up my spine. My breathing became erratic as he traced his finger along the tie that was holding my robe closed.

"Nick," I said in a breathy voice.

"Yeah, I know you have...Bobby." he spat his name out as if it were spoiled against his tongue. "You know I'm the better man, right?"

Nick wrapped his arm around my waist and pulled me close to him. The whisky fuming off of him was so intense I could've easily gotten drunk with a simple taste of his tongue. I tried to pull away from him but if I were being honest, I wasn't fighting very hard. He tilted my head back and ran his tongue up the center of my neck. A moan escaped my lips, and I could feel his thick dick pressing against my thighs.

"Nicky!" an auburn skinned woman sang as she opened his room door. She held herself up as she gripped the door and I realized she was just as drunk as he was.

Her short black hair was pulled back in a messy ponytail exposing her long neck and enormous hoop earrings. She had on one black high heel and a skintight halter top dress that showed off her petite body. She leaned against the door frame and seductively called Nick's name again as she pulled down the top of her dress letting everyone get a view of her bouncy B-cup breasts.

"Just say the word and I'll get rid of her ass," Nick whispered in my ear. I attempted to push off of him, but he tightened his grip.

"Nicky, baby, what are you doing over there with – eww - her?" the woman said as she eyed me in disgust.

Embarrassment hit me in the gut as I pushed Nick off of me. I glared at the woman, but she just smirked and rolled her eyes. Not wanting her to have the satisfaction of seeing the tears flooding my vision, I slammed the door in their faces. I leaned my head against the door and let out a muffled cry. I wanted nothing more than to crawl into a hole and disappear. Why the hell did I think that Nick actually was attracted to me? I mean, he only touched me because he was clearly drunk. He obviously had a type – thin and beautiful. I was neither of those.

"C'mon baby," the woman purred.

I looked through the peephole and I could see the hurt stained on his face as he stared at my room door, his hands balled into tight fists. The woman suddenly stepped in front of him breaking his trance and wrapped his hands around her. She pulled his face to hers and impatiently tried to kiss him, but he jerked his head away. He picked her up and threw her over his shoulder like it was nothing. Taking one last glance at my room and stormed to his.

I ran to the bathroom and shoved my toothbrush down my throat.

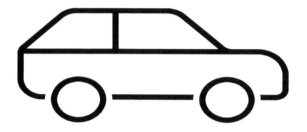

Chapter 19

Nicholas

The taste of Ashlynn invaded my tastebuds, and I couldn't stomach to have Jasmine – shit or Katlin, hell I couldn't remember her name but whoever this woman was - licking all over me. She needed to go. I wanted her ass out of my room so that I could get back to Ashlynn.

"What's wrong baby?" she cooed as she flicked her tongue against my ear.

"I think you should go," I said, rubbing my eyes.

She sat up straight and looked down. She folded her arms, and a scoff escaped her lips. She was straddled on my lap and butt ass naked. "That's some bullshit."

"Look, I'm just not into it like I thought I was."

"Liar!" she accused as she reached under her and pointed at my hard dick. "You fucking want me. I didn't come all this way to not get fucked."

"C'mon on Jasmine," I said, attempting to get up.

"It's Monica!" she said, shoving me back onto the bed and placing her hands on her hips.

Oops, I wasn't even close. I shrugged with indifference and placed my hands behind my head. I should just fuck her. It was all she was good for, and I needed to release some of this backed up pressure.

Shit, the only reason I brought her back to my room was so that I could get Ashlynn out of my system. I needed to remind myself what most women were good for and to jog my memory that they could not be trusted. Hell, I've already caught this bitch looking through my pants pockets when she thought I wasn't paying attention.

If I recalled, even Ashlynn's ass was looking through my wallet. *Yeah, that's right*, I thought. Ashlynn ass may have that sweet innocent role laid out, but she could not be trusted either.

"Get on your knees," I demanded.

She flashed a wicked smile as she climbed off of me. Positing herself in between my legs, she took me in her hands and flicked her tongue against the tip of my head. Her hot breath tingled in my balls as she attempted to fully put me in her mouth. Her eyes widened as she realized I was too thick for her mouth and she began to gag. I grabbed the back of her head and shoved my dick deeper down her throat. The rush of saliva coated my dick and I let out a groan.

"Damn nigga!" she coughed, slapping my hand off her head.

I peered down at her and laughed. "What happened to all that freaky shit you were spitting at me at the bar? What happened to 'I don't gag' shit?" I said, mocking her.

"Fuck you!" she spat, getting back onto her feet. "I don't have to take this shit."

I smacked my lips and sat up on my forearms. "You mad because you don't know how to suck dick? Grow up."

"Go have that fat bitch across the hall suck your dick!" She yelled, throwing her hands in the air.

I jumped up from the bed and glared down at her. Except for what I was going to do to Olivia when I caught up to her, I would never hurt a female. The rage that was pouring out of me was about to throw my morals out the window.

"Don't you ever, in your miserable fucking life say some shit like that again -especially if I'm around. She didn't do anything to your trifling ass. How fucking insecure are you to bring another harmless woman down? Like I said, grow the fuck up and get the fuck out."

Monica's breath caught as she took several feet away from me. I took slow shallow breaths as my chest heaved from fury. I glowered at her and counted in my head to keep myself from doing her any harm. Ashlynn wasn't here to defend herself so I would, especially from this irrelevant broad.

" Whatever, you're just a bitch nigga anyway." She mumbled as she gathered her clothes off the floor.

I nodded and held the door open for her. She bumped past me and stormed down the hallway cursing me out. I couldn't have given two fucks and slammed my room door. I sat on the bed and rested my head in my hands. I was completely lost. A part of me wanted to bang on Ashlynn's door and devour her in bed. The other part of me wanted to keep her in a distance.

"She's engaged. She's engaged. She's engaged, "I repeated out loud pounding my fist against my knee.

What the fuck was my problem? Not only was my idiotic heart trying to fall for someone who was off limits, but it was trying to fall for someone period. I couldn't let that shit happen, not again. I refused to be betrayed and have my heart stomped on. Or, in my case, have a bullet in it. I grimaced as my fingers brushed against the menacing scar that permanently resided on my chest.

Letting another woman come close to me was doomed to end in tragedy. Besides, who was I kidding? Even if I humored myself and pursued Ashlynn, it wouldn't have worked. I'm damaged goods and she deserved somebody who could give her the world. I wasn't that man. I disrespected so many women over the past two years like it was second nature. I didn't deserve anybody but my own demons.

I grabbed the whisky bottle off of the nightstand and gulped the last of it. I savored the burning sensation that hit my chest and laid back on the bed. Closing my eyes, I made the decision to stick with my plan.

I'd be cordial with Ashlynn but keep all secular thoughts to myself. Once I made it to Vegas, I'd depart from her and never look back.

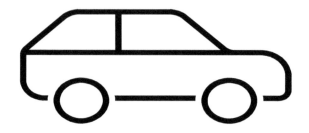

Chapter 20

Ashlynn

I pounded on Nick's door for the second time this morning. I let him slide at seven because it was still pretty early. I grabbed a banana from the complimentary breakfast bar and took a stroll along the pier. The sun gradually ascended, casting hues of pink and orange across the wide sky. Its golden rays danced freely against the dark water. I took a moment to pray and compliment God on his breathtaking creation.

An hour passed once I made it back to the hotel and tried knocking on Nick's door again. Still, no answer – only the deep snores coming from behind the door reassured me that he was still there. I went back into my room and double checked all my belongings were packed in my bag. My phone chimed indicating a new notification. I walked over to the nightstand, and I saw my dad's picture on display.

Dad: *Ashlynn, call me when you get a chance. I want to go over a few things concerning the shops and my expectations for when you and Bobby take over.*

Huh? What was he talking about? Bobby said my dad only casually brought up the idea of us taking over earlier than anticipated. I immediately dialed my dad's number.

"I thought you were driving?" My dad asked.

"Uh-no I had a late start. I'm assuming Bobby told you I was driving that way instead of flying," I stated with confirmation.

"Yeah," my dad grunted before mumbling under his breath.

"What's wrong?"

"I-uh," he sighed heavily and cleared his throat. "I just don't think it was a good idea for you to be driving across the damn country by yourself."

"I know, but Bobby and I agreed that he should stay behind for the inspection today."

"Damn that! Now I like Bobby, but as a man, he should be with you. God forbid something terrible happens to you and you're alone."

I stared at my phone to make sure I was actually talking to my dad. Was I hearing him correctly? Dare I say that he was actually sticking up for me?

"Dad?"

"I'm sorry sweetheart - to be honest with you, I still get anxious about getting behind the wheel. Ever since your mom and grandma died in that car accident, I've hated driving. So for you to be driving such a long way, has me on pins and needles."

"You never told me that, Dad."

"Being here with your granddad has had me thinking about a lot of things. I know you and I haven't gotten along for a while, and I know how hard I've been on you. I just wanted you to want for nothing. I wanted you to have the best education so you would never have to struggle like me and your mom did before we had you."

"I hated how hard you were on me growing up. I hated that you pushed me away when Mom died. I was only seven and it felt like you didn't want me around - that's why I leaned so much on Grandpa. He wanted the best for me, but he always took the time to acknowledge me. You didn't. I felt as if I was never good enough for you." I said, a tear escaping my eyes.

"I've always been proud of you Ashlynn and I've always loved you. I am sorry."

I grunted. "I appreciate you apologizing, and I will forgive you – it'll just take some time."

"That's understandable. As I said, watching your grandfather go through all of these extensive tests for a life-threatening disease made me realize how short our time on this earth is. I was hurting when we lost Mom, but that gave me no right to treat you and my dad the way I did. You two were my only family and I pushed y'all away. I'm going to try and make things right while I still have breath in my body."

My eyes burned with more tears. I could hear the genuine care in my dad's voice and for the first time, I was excited to see him. Yes, I was still upset about how he'd treated me over the years, but he was going to try to make things right. Who wouldn't want that? Besides, I didn't like carrying this grudge and anger against him. I just wanted him to love and be proud of me.

My dad cleared his throat and sniffed. "Now, let's talk about you taking over the business," my dad said, a smile booming in his voice. "Bobby told me that you were on board for me to transfer everything over to you all by the summer."

"What?" I said in shock.

"Didn't you and Bobby already talk about this? He told me y'all did and to call him later today. I figured I'd call you since I knew his hands were going to be full with the inspections."

What the hell was Bobby doing? How could he agree for us to take over the shops without talking to me about it first? I mean, yes, he knew I had hardly any interest in the automotive business, but this was still my family's business.

"Uh, it must've slipped my mind," I lied. I wasn't up for handling business so early in the morning and I for damn sure didn't want to ruin the bond my dad and I were starting to form. "Dad, sorry I want to hit the road so I can make it there by the end of the day tomorrow."

"Tomorrow? I hope you're taking breaks and not forcing yourself to drive for long periods of time with no sleep."

I chewed my bottom lip and contemplated whether I should tell my dad about Nick. Not wanting to piss off my dad or send him into a panic attack, I thought against it. "Don't worry, I'm resting and not driving when I'm tired. I'll call you a bit later. I love you."

"Okay baby girl, I love you too."

We disconnected the call, and I couldn't help but smile. It was the first time that my dad and I talked on the phone for longer than five minutes without arguing. It didn't mean that everything was peachy, but it was definitely a start. Who knows, maybe he'd understand that I didn't want to run his business but run my own instead. I checked the time and shot up off the bed. It was after nine now and we were way behind from hitting the road.

I grabbed my bag and hotel key and stormed across the hall. I banged on Nick's door. After a few minutes, I heard him curse as he scrambled into the room. He swung the door open with aggravation. His face softened when he realized it was me.

"Lynn, what can I do for you?" Nick asked with a yawn. He stretched and my eyes glued to his abdomen. How I wanted to trail my tongue down his body. Wait! What the hell was I thinking, he already had that slim woman doing that.

"It's late – we need to get on the road so we can make it to Vegas by tomorrow," I said nonchalantly tapping my foot.

He grimaced and rubbed his hand down his face. "What time is it?"

"After nine. I'll drive the first leg, just get your shit so we can check out and get on the road."

"Shit," he grumbled. "Give me 45 minutes and I'll meet you downstairs."

I nodded, keeping a blank expression on my face, and walked away. I didn't want to take my chances to see the woman still sprawled out on his bed. I checked out of my room and waited outside in the car.

The thought of his wet tongue gliding up my neck intruded my mind. Ugh! Why didn't I stop him? Who am I kidding? I secretly wanted him to do that from the minute I opened the door and saw his bare chest. I was ready to risk it all for him if it weren't for that woman interrupting us. I was no match for her anyway. Once it was said and done, I knew that Nick was going to choose her over me last night.

Shaking my head, I picked up my phone and texted Bobby. I knew he wouldn't answer being he was at work, but I just wanted to tell him I loved him. I needed to tell him to remind myself that I was engaged. Who Nick fucked was not my concern.

Exactly 45 minutes later, Nick sluggishly walked out of the hotel sipping on a large cup of coffee. He had on a plain black shirt and a pair of gray sweats with Nike slides. His usually neat locs were tied up in a disheveled bun. Even though he had on a pair of dark glasses, he winced at the bright sun.

He sank into the passenger seat and leaned his head back on the headrest. He looked at me over his shoulder and smiled weakly. "Everybody hates Mondays, right?"

I rolled my eyes and backed out of the parking lot.

We spent the next few hours listening to music in silence. Every now and then I'd catch him looking in my direction, but he didn't utter a word. Not that I cared, but it was becoming extremely awkward. We still had a day and a half to be together and there was no way we were going to complete this trip uncomfortably.

I opened my mouth to say something, but Nick had already passed back out. I sighed in relief and turned on the Audible book I picked out last night. At least I could step into a made-up world of spice and romance, and leave my reality behind for a while.

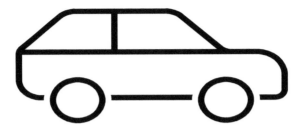

Chapter 21

Nicholas

The vexing drum against my temples finally subdued when I opened my eyes. My mouth was dry, and I was in dire need of water. I sat up and rolled my shoulders as I stretched. I looked over to see that Ashlynn was gone. I panicked for a brief moment when I realized that we were stopped at a gas station.

"I moaned as his dick slammed against my walls."

"What the fuck?" I said, staring at the radio. *Dick Pleaser* scrolled on the screen for display, and it took everything in me to not burst out in laughter.

Ashlynn had left her audiobook playing as she went inside the store. I stroked my beard and laughed. This woman kept surprising me. I remembered she said she liked reading smutty romance stories, but I didn't think she'd let a book play while I was in the car.

Ashlynn came back to the car and in pure amusement, I watched as her eyes widened in horror. She fumbled through her purse, retrieving her phone to turn off the book as I covered my mouth to hold back a laugh.

"Ashlynn, Ashlynn, Ashlynn," I playfully tsked at her. "What have you been doing while I've been sleeping?"

"Oh, shut up," she pouted, rolling her eyes. "I wasn't doing anything but listening to my book."

"Well, I hope whoever was getting their walls smashed in was enjoying it."

We stared at each other for a moment before bursting out in laughter. The tension seemed to dissolve between us, and relief lifted off my shoulders. Ashlynn wiped away a tear as she held her stomach and tried to catch her breath.

"About last night," I started, but she held up her hand. I gently moved it down. "I apologize for invading you and your personal space without consent. I had been drinking and I- "

"And things just got carried away? No worries. I know when I get drunk, I tend to do or say things I don't mean," she laughed, interrupting me.

I cocked my head to the side, "I wasn't going to say that. I meant what I said to you last night. If you would've said the word, I would've thrown that bitch out sooner than when I did."

She visibly swallowed. "Wh-what? You actually wanted to…" her voice trailed off as she hesitantly looked at me. She cleared her throat and shook her head. "Wait, you kicked her out of your room?"

I drummed my fingers against my thigh and exhaled. "Yeah, I did."

"Oh. Was it because she saw what we were doing?" she nervously asked.

"I could care less who saw me," I snapped.

Ashlynn flinched and pressed her lips together. I puffed out my breath and ran my sweaty hands down my pants.

"Lynn, I apologize. It's just…you're making it extremely hard for me to focus. You are a distraction."

"What are you trying to stay focused on that I am supposedly distracting you from?" she asked irritably.

I looked down and scowled. Okay, that was definitely a poor choice of words on my end. Shit, it's been a while since I tried to make friends. I took a deep breath and looked back at her.

"Last night, I found myself wanting to be closer to you, and I realize that trying to seduce you was without a doubt the wrong approach. I can admit that I am attracted to you, but I shouldn't have put you in that uncomfortable situation. Now if you weren't engaged and I didn't have that silly broad with me, well, that's a different story."

I watched as Ashlynn tried to hide the smile creeping across her face. She licked her lips and took a deep breath. "That's how I'm distracting you?"

I nodded. "I need to stay focus on my plan while I head to Vegas. It's hard for me to trust anybody, especially women. The two most important ones in my life fucked me over and I promised myself I wouldn't let another woman get close to me again." I started.

Ashlynn's lips turn downward into a frown. "You don't trust women at all?"

I shook my head.

"What happened to you?" she asked.

I shifted uneasily in my seat. The urge to keep my wall up was being torn down brick by brick when it came to Ashlynn. What if she turned her nose up at me once she found out how I grew up? What if I did tell her and she used the pain from my past against me? Then again, my time with her was limited. So what I told her about my past? It's not like I'd see her again after tomorrow. I swallowed.

I think that was the part that was scaring me the most right now. In just two days, this woman has me obsessing over her. I find myself yearning to know more about who she is, what makes her sad, what makes her happy, her dreams and goals, and what she tastes like. Especially what she tastes like, but in twelve hours she'd be out of my life. A part of me didn't care, but the other part was devastated.

Fuck it! I'll tell her and if she judged me, then leaving her would have no effect on me. This schoolboy crush would be thrown in the toilet and I could get back to focusing on my plan.

I sighed, "My mother turned me and my older brother over to a life of drug dealing when I was eight years old."

"What!" Ashlynn exclaimed in shock.

Shrugging my shoulders, I turned to face her. Her face was scrunched up with a mixture of anger and confusion.

"I didn't know any better and believed her when she said it was just a fun game that we were going to play. Once we started having ample amounts of food, clothes, and toys in the house, I really thought we were winning. I used to ask her how she was playing the game too if Garrett and I were always collecting and dropping off bags and getting all of the presents."

I chuckled, "She only laughed at me and told me not to worry about it. I only needed to do what T, our drug boss, instructed. As long as he was happy, we could all keep playing the game.

"On Garrett's fifteenth birthday, T changed up the routine to have us move cocaine rocks instead of weed. Even at thirteen, I knew how dangerous that was going to be. Not only was cocaine a higher price, meaning we'd be bigger targets to get robbed, but it was a bigger sentence in jail if we'd ever got caught with any of the product on us. The night I tried to voice my concerns to my mom, I was hit in the gut with absolute disgust. T was sitting on the edge of my mother's bed while she was in between his legs. When she saw me, she laughed and said this was how she was winning the game."

I swallowed the lump in my throat and dug my nails in the palm of my hands. She tried to convince T to have us move more than just weed so that she could get a bigger cut of the money. When he refused, she whored herself out in exchange for getting any drug she wanted at half the price.

"I never told anyone what I saw that night. I couldn't stomach the thought." I continued but kept my eyes straight ahead of me. "I watched my mom do unspeakable things just to get her fix. I remember being so afraid that she'd stoop low enough to sell us over to T permanently like some of the desperate parents did when they wanted drugs."

Ashlynn flinched.

I sighed and shook my head. T had a reputation for adopting kids in exchange for the parents to get whichever drug was their kryptonite. I remember seeing kids as young as six months old being given to one of T's mistresses so they could be raised under his rule. When my mom was angry that we hadn't made enough money, she had no problem threatening me and Garrett with the promise of allowing T to adopt us. My mother had ruined our childhood by getting all of us caught up in a world of drugs.

"Nick," Ashlynn whispered as she stared at me with sorrow.

"Don't take pity on me. When I turned eighteen, my brother and I finally got out of my mom's house and into a place of our own."

I held up my wallet. "The woman in this picture had been by my side through high school. She made me believe that she cared for me and didn't care about the type of life I lived. She covered for me and had my back. So, when she agreed to move in with us, I was ecstatic. I thought I was happy and in love. I'd finally found a woman that I could trust, and I gave her my heart. She betrayed me."

I looked Ashlynn in the eyes. "She's the one who got my brother killed. And to put the icing on the cake, she's the one who shot me."

"Oh, my God, Nick. That's awful!" She reached for me but hesitated. "I'm sorry I know you said not to pity you, but I really want to give you a fucking hug."

I smirked as I stared at her. Her face was full of pain and sorrow for me. As much as I didn't want to, it felt good to talk about the bullshit I'd been through. I got out of the car and walked around to her side. I pulled her out of the driver's seat with an embrace. She wrapped her arms around my upper back and squeezed.

The realization that she wasn't judging me or calling me weak for being vulnerable had my heart stuttering. I rested my chin on top of her head and held her against me. I guess two things were missing in my life – my revenge and a friend.

"I didn't mean to put all of this on you. It's just…I don't know. I feel at ease when you're around. Like I can put my guard down and tell you everything."

"I guess it was time you trusted in somebody again – especially in a female like me," she joked, looking up at me.

"Yeah, I guess so," I said staring into her affectionate eyes.

I stared at her lips and wanted nothing more than to taste them. Ashlynn had my heart in a chokehold, and she didn't even know it.

"So," she said, stepping away from me. "Ready to hit the road? We have twenty more hours before we reach Vegas. So, I was thinking if we –"

I didn't hear anything she was saying as my eyes roamed down her curved body. The flowy black dress she had on showed off her scrumptious breasts and wide hips. Her hair was pulled back into a ponytail exposing her cute ears that I wanted to nibble on. She smiled at me, exposing her dimples, and I couldn't take it anymore.

I gently grabbed Ashlynn by her elbow and pulled her to me. Pressing her body against mine, I stared down at her. The sweet scent of coca butter filled my nose. I swallowed before leaning down and capturing her lips. Her sweet soft lips had me in a trance. I haven't kissed anybody since Olivia – it was too intimate. Fucking Ashlynn was making me break my own rule.

Her eyes widened with shock, but she didn't pull away from me. I held her tighter and flicked my tongue against her lips, waiting for her to open up to me. She slowly parted her lips and welcomed my tongue. Relaxing, she moaned and wrapped her hands around my neck. The desire I had for her coursed through my body, causing me to kiss her harder. I felt my dick harden against my sweatpants and by the way she grinded against me, I knew she felt it.

"Stop," Ashlynn said, breaking our kiss. She leaned against the car and tried to catch her breath. "I'm sorry Nick, I can't. I'm getting married."

I shook my head, "I took advantage of your kindness."

"No no, I took advantage of you! I mean, I know you were just trying to open up and talk to a friend. Besides, I didn't stop you."

We stared at each other, and by the way she was fidgeting, I could tell she didn't really want us to stop. Hell, I didn't either. All I wanted to do now was find us a hotel and pull her dress up over her ass so I could dive my tongue in between her legs. I shook my head and grinned at her.

"Let's just forget that ever happened. How about I drive for a bit? Where are we anyway?" I asked, rambling off questions.

"Just outside of Cedar Rapids," Ashlynn said, handing me the keys. "We can be in Colorado in the next ten hours, but it'll be just after midnight."

"Do you want to drive that late?" I asked, opening the passenger door for her.

"Not really, but once we make it through Colorado, Vegas is only a nine-hour drive away. You'd be able to meet up with whoever you had planned to see by tomorrow night if we keep driving."

I closed the passenger door for her with a faint grin and walked to the driver's side. "Dammit," I grumbled to myself. I had really fucked that up. Why the hell did I kiss her? Ashlynn had made up her mind last night – she wasn't going to leave Bobby. I was dumb to think she would. I needed to end this pointless crush I had on her, especially since I knew it wasn't going to bloom into anything special.

Ashlynn was the first woman I wanted to keep close to me in a long while. No, I couldn't have her to myself, but her friendship would suffice. After I handled Olivia in Vegas, maybe I could meet back up with her in California or back home in Philly. It didn't matter to me, as long as we stayed friends – and nothing more.

"I'll get us to Colorado," I promised, hopping into the driver's seat.

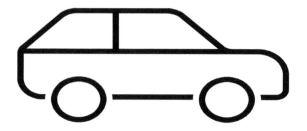

Chapter 22

Ashlynn

Why did Nick have to kiss me? Why did he have to kiss me with so much passion that put Bobby's simple pecks to shame?

Fuck I wanted to feel his lips on mine again, but what would that say about me? How could I keep turning Nick down with the excuse that I was getting married, and yet, I still fantasized about him? I didn't stop him not once, but twice now when he placed his lips on me. I couldn't deny it – I wanted him. Even if it were for one night, but I was not a cheater. I could never betray Bobby by sleeping with someone else – no matter how much I wanted to.

With each stop between Iowa and Nebraska, I found it harder to stick with my morals. Nick was kind and made me laugh. I found myself wanting to know more about him. Not just sexually, but mentally. We had so much in common, from our favorite types of food that we explored through each state we passed through to the type of music we listened to while driving. I knew there was still hurt from his past lingering, but I could tell that wasn't affecting him anymore.

I sighed and texted Bobby for the tenth time before setting my phone down. I hadn't spoken with him since we left Chicago. It was well after 9 p.m. and there was no way that he was still at work, but he hadn't responded to me yet. I don't know what's been going on with him, but it was starting to piss me off and worry me. I'd been on the road for two going on three days now, and he's hardly checked in on me.

How could a fiancé go for days without talking to their future wife knowing they were driving for hours at a time? Was he having an affair? No, no way! I mean, I'd know, right? The thought of Bobby having another woman in our bed had my stomach churning.

Nick started to sing along to Tevin Campbell's Can We Talk, and I couldn't help but smile. His voice turned me on – singing or not. My thoughts started to fill with impurity and my smile quickly faded when I realized how hypocritical I was being. I was thinking the worst and accusing Bobby of cheating while I was over here allowing another man to kiss on me. I was playing with fire and if I wasn't careful, I would lose Bobby.

I stiffened when my phone vibrated with a text notification. I shook my head and smiled, allowing myself to relax when I saw Bobby's name on the screen. I, once again, was overreacting and letting my mind get away from me. I needed to stop thinking about Nick and keep my focus on my future husband.

I opened the message from Bobby, but there weren't any words - only emojis. My heart pounded against my chest as I stared at a group of pictures that were in the form of an equation - pig plus candy equals red x, broken heart, and sad face. A second message popped up, this time with a girl running plus broccoli equals green check mark, happy face, a wedding ring, and a tongue with water splashes next to it.

"What's wrong?" Nick asked, gazing over at me.

I ignored him as my mind raced at warp speed. I tried to process what Bobby was saying to me through fucking pictures like he was a damn child instead of just using his words.

Apparently, I was a pig and only ate junk food, so I was going to end up with a broken heart. However, if I worked out and ate health-ily, then we'd be married and we'd have more oral sex. I'm assuming he meant more sex in general since I was constantly begging him for intimacy.

It was taking everything in me to not throw my phone out the window as steam seeped through my head. Why would he send me some shit like this? He ignores me the majority of the day and when he does finally text me back, it has to do with me losing weight.

My hurt dropped to the pit of my stomach with the realization that it was all my fault. I tried to swallow the lump forming in my throat but found I was failing – fast.

"Pull the car over," I whispered, feeling the bile burn.

"What?"

"Please, pull the car over," I shouted, reaching for the door handle.

Nick skidded to the side of the road as I yanked the door open. I jumped out of the car and hurled in the tall grass. Tears stung my eyes as the lunch Nick, and I had earlier released onto the ground. My heart ached with pain as the constant reminder of my body flooded my mind.

I loved Bobby and I know he loves me too, but I messed things up. I overate and didn't exercise as consistently as I needed. Hell, I had gained a total of thirty pounds since we'd been together – no wonder he was disgusted with me.

"Whoa!" Nick gasped as he watched me shove my finger down my throat. I didn't mean for him to see me, but what did I care? After tomorrow, he'd be the only one who knew my secret.

"I have to be skinnier. It's the only way to guarantee my marriage is a success," I said through tears. "He'll love me more if I just stop eating so much. He'll go back to paying attention to me if I just lost twenty pounds."

I tried to force myself to hurl again, but Nick grabbed my arms and pinned them down to my side. The road was dark except for the headlights beaming, but the moon was full, allowing me to see the look of rage spreading across Nick's face.

"You've got to be fucking kidding me, Ashlynn! Who the fuck put that bullshit in your head?" he asked, his jaw ticking.

When I didn't answer, he shook my shoulders and asked me again. I gazed down as my tears flowed harder down my face and I kept my mouth closed. I was too humiliated to face Nick.

"I swear if it was your bitch ass fiancé…" Nick huffed, before letting go of me.

He stomped back to the car and for a moment I thought he was getting back in so we could continue driving. Instead, he retrieved a couple of napkins and a water bottle. My eyes widened as he gingerly began to clean my face and hands. He handed me the water bottle and instructed me to rinse out my mouth. I took the bottle from him with shaky hands, causing lines to form in between his brows.

He ran his hands through his hair and observed me – the look of anger softened, and sadness replaced it. He tried to meet my eyes, but I turned away, ashamed of how pitiful and disgusted I was with myself. How could Nick have even remotely been attracted to me the other night when I looked like this? The woman he had in his room was beautiful and thin while I wasn't.

"Look at me," Nick demanded, cupping his finger under my chin. I reluctantly met his eyes and saw something looming behind them - he was genuinely hurt. "You are fucking beautiful! I wish you could step into my shoes and see what I see when I look at you. Bobby is a gotdamn fool for not telling you how breathtaking you are. I've never met anyone as cool, funny, sweet, and sexy as you."

"You're just saying that to make me feel better," I mumbled, trying to pull away from him, but he wrapped an arm around my waist and held on to me.

"You have no idea how amazing you are and it fucking sucks that you don't see that. Don't rely on anybody – especially a man, including me – to tell you that. So what you have a cute belly! You deserve someone who isn't embarrassed to love you or that tries to change you to satisfy their own selfish needs."

I looked into his unblinking concerned eyes. "You think my belly is cute?"

He chuckled and rubbed the middle of my back, "Hell yeah! Everything about you is, well, let's just say it's hard for me to not think some specific thoughts – especially since you're committed to your fi-ancé."

My face warmed and I felt an overwhelming sensation of shy-ness as I stood close to him. A wave of butterflies swam through my core causing a shiver to run up my spine. Bobby's never said anything so nice to me even when we first started dating.

Now here Nick was who's barely known me, and he's already made me feel like I was this one-of-a-kind type of woman. I knew my self-confidence was shit and I had work to do on myself. Being around Nick these last couple of days has given me the type of courage to seek out therapy and find self-love.

"Ready to hit the road slim thick?" Nick asked, playfully poking me in the side. I giggled and nodded. Nick reached out his hand and I gladly took it.

Maybe it was time to move on from Bobby. I mean Nick was right, I don't want to be with anybody who's going to make me feel like crap about how I look. I knew what type of woman I was, and I knew how I wanted to be loved. What Bobby has been showing me for the past year was not it. If he didn't want to be with me anymore, then I'd rather he'd tell me like a man instead of saying cruel things to me and pushing me away.

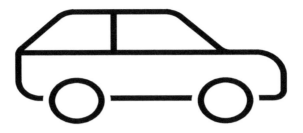

Chapter 23

Nicholas

If I ever met that bitch ass nigga Bobby, I was going to knock his head off. Watching Ashlynn make herself throw up because of what he constantly told her about her weight made me want to turn the car around and head back to Philly.

I looked over at Ashlynn who was fast asleep in the passenger seat. She deserved so much better – hell, she deserved the gotdamn world, but she didn't even realize it. Her confidence had been shaken down so badly that she started to believe the lies spewing in her ear. It made me sick to my fucking stomach, but I had less than a day left with her. I don't know how much of an influence I could have on her, but hopefully, she'd remember what I was telling her.

I was starting to realize that Ashlynn was not like most females. She was actually sweet and didn't care about what was in my bank account. I couldn't count how many times she went out of her way to buy me lunch or snacks whenever we stopped. Olivia's bitch ass had my wallet or made sure I gave her a minimum of five hundred in cash whenever she walked out of the house.

"The Aspen Resort," I read out loud as I passed the sign. I glanced over at Lynn again and merged across the highway to exit toward the resort. Tomorrow we'd be in Vegas, and I wanted Ashlynn to have one more relaxing day before we parted ways.

After another thirty-minute drive, I pulled into the resort parking lot near the entrance and made sure the doors were locked before heading inside. I was instantly in awe of the luxurious atmosphere that was adorned with rustic décor. An emerald water fountain fluttered lightly in the middle of the foyer and was surrounded by fall decorations. I could hear the soft melodies of a piano and glasses clinking behind double wooden doors to my right and figured it was a bar. To my left was a long hall leading to elevators and the spa area. I instantly felt cozy and just knew that Ashlynn would enjoy her night here.

"Welcome sir, how can I help?" an older woman smiled at me from behind the front desk. She had her feathery gray hair pinned back into a low bun and her glasses were sitting at the edge of her nose.

"Hi, I know it's a bit last minute, but do you happen to have two rooms available for this evening?" I asked, smiling back at her.

"Let me see what we have." After a few clicks from her computer, her lips turned into a slight frown. "I am sorry sir, we do not have two rooms available tonight."

My shoulders slumped and I dipped my chin with a half-hearted smile before turning to leave.

"Sir, wait!" the front desk clerk called out. "It looks like you've been driving for a while, and I'd hate to turn away a customer. I do have a private villa behind the resort available if you don't mind a two-night minimum at five hundred dollars a night."

I turned back toward her and rubbed the back of my neck. "Two nights minimum? How big is the villa?"

"Well, it's a spacious and private secluded studio that comes with a California King bed, living and dining area with a kitchenette. Also, a private patio overlooking the mountain along with a heated jacuzzi. It's a very romantic spot for you and your partner. The couple that originally booked the room was on the fence about coming here and with it being well after midnight, it's safe to   assume that they are not coming."

"Thank you, Ruth," I said looking at her name tag, "but I'm just traveling with a friend and that may be too romantic. I really appreciate your offer though."

"Oh, I apologize dear, I did not mean to assume. I can still offer the villa for you both if you don't mind an open layout. There is a pull-out sofa in the living room area and I can have someone bring up a dividing panel for privacy."

"Wow, that would be amazing!" I said, cheering up. Of course, there were plenty of other hotels we could've stayed in, but I wanted Ashlynn to enjoy the little bit of time we had left together.

After paying for the room and receiving a copy of the key, I darted back to the car to see Ashlynn playing solitaire on her phone.

"Where are we?" she asked, as I got back in the car.

"I thought you could use some rest in a real bed and take some time to relax. The plan was for you to spend a day at the spa and we hit the road tomorrow, but there was a two night minimum for the villa."

"Two nights?" Ashlynn asked, sitting straight up in her seat. "Nick, I have to get to Cali, and did you say villa? Those are extremely expensive; I can't let you waste money on me like that."

"Lynn," I said, resting my hand on her shoulder, "it's okay. For one, I am not worried about the cost. You deserve to be pampered, especially with all of the stress and bullshit you've been going through lately. Second of all, I know you have to get to Cali to see your grandpa, so if you like – which I hope not – you can go ahead and leave tomorrow, while I finish the drive to Vegas in a rental car on Thursday."

A smile formed on her lips as she relaxed back into her seat. "This was really sweet of you Nick, to go out of your way for me."

"No sweat, like I said you deserve it. Self-love and self-care are crucial in anyone's life. There is one more thing," I started, taking my hand off of her shoulder. "The villa is a private studio with only one bed. I don't mind sleeping on the couch and the clerk said she can have room panels sent so you can have your privacy. If that's not enough, I can get a room at the hotel a few miles away. You can - "

"Nick!" she interrupted with a chuckle, resting her hand on mine. "It's okay. I don't mind sharing the room with you. A room divider should give us more than enough privacy."

I smiled and nodded my head as I drove us behind the resort. The villa was just as the clerk said, secluded and overlooking the snowy mountain. I hoped that Ashlynn wouldn't get freaked out. Yes, we'd spent the last two going on three days together, but never in an isolated sleeping space. The moment she said she was uncomfortable; I was getting my black ass out of there.

A small gasp escaped Ashlynn when we stepped inside. The private studio was nestled with lush surroundings and a welcoming warmth that instantly wrapped around us. A combination of deep gray and burgundy color palettes decorated the room. A compact kitchenette stood ready for culinary endeavors and was fully stocked with a few premium liquor choices. To our left was the California king bed dressed up with a matching burgundy comforter and gray sheets.

I swallowed as the intimate retreat overwhelmed me. The place was amazing, but I was starting to realize that I was going to be here alone with Ashlynn with a full shelf of liquor. I shook my head and ignored the thought of us getting into bed together. I know she wouldn't allow it. Besides, she'll have her day booked with going to the spa, going shopping, and whatever she wanted to do. We'd only be together alone in the room at night when we slept. Then, she'd be gone tomorrow afternoon.

"This place is really nice Nick," Ashlynn stated playfully bumping into my arm. "I smell gross, and I know my breath is rank from earlier, so I'm going to hit up the bathroom first."

I chuckled as she walked off. I walked back outside to retrieve our bags from the trunk when a set of headlights started heading in my direction. I squinted my eyes and prepared to beat somebody's ass when I noticed it was a man driving the resort's golf cart with panels hanging out of the back.

"Good evening, or morning sir," the young man said stopping in front of me.

"How are you doing man?" I asked helping him take out the room dividers and walked them inside the villa.

"I'm not dead or in jail, so no complaining on my end. I'm blessed with a job and roof over my head," he said in a chipper voice.

I chuckled, "I like that answer. What's your name?"

"Nathan but everyone calls me Nate."

"Well, Nate, keep that same positive attitude throughout your life. As a young black man, sometimes people only want to see you fail in life or make you a statistic. Just keep saving yo' bread and start investing your time and money on things that'll make you happy and not on women. They can be your biggest downfall."

A concerned look crossed Nate's face as he sat the last divider down in the living room. He opened his mouth to say something but quickly shut it. I arched an eyebrow as he shifted his weight from foot to foot. It looked like he was fighting the urge to hold his tongue. He stopped fidgeting and squared his shoulders before placing his hand on my shoulder.

"Sir, if I may, you have to let go of the past. I know you don't know me, but something is telling me to tell you that everything's going to be okay if you just let go. Remember what the Bible says in 1 Peter 3:9: Do not repay evil with evil or insult with insult."

My mouth flew open as I stared at him. For the first time in a long time, I was at a loss for words. Now, I am still new in my faith, and I've heard people say that God has ways of speaking to you, but I was finding that hard to believe. I mean if that were the case, he would've been talking to a lot of corrupt people and stopping them from making horrible decisions. The world would be a totally different place.

Now I was starting to realize that maybe he had been trying to speak to me, but through other people – and I've just been too stubborn to listen. Ayzo was telling me to not seek out Olivia, I've heard countless sermons about forgiveness, and now this complete stranger was talking to me about letting go of the past and not seeking out revenge.

I swallowed the lump in my throat and took a few deep breaths. "Thanks, man. That was a word that I had been running away from and refusing to accept for a long time now."

A grin formed on Nate's face as he clapped my back, "Trust in God's plan, he's always going to have your back sir."

I nodded and watched as he turned to leave. "Wait, let me give you a tip."

"No thanks, seeing that I've done both of my jobs is reward enough. Have a blessed day." Nate said with a grin and left.

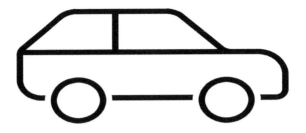

Chapter 24

Ashlynn

I felt ten times better once I stepped out of the shower. Twelve hours in a car with a two-hour period of smelling like sweat and vomit could make even the least hygienic individual appreciate a hot shower. I grabbed one of the complimentary toothbrush and toothpaste packets out of the top drawer before brushing my teeth.

Once I was done, I hesitated to leave the bathroom. I mean, the bathroom was equipped with two complimentary bathrobes, but I didn't want to walk around naked with just a robe. The last time I had a robe on around Nick flashed through my mind. The way his hands were mere seconds from untying it and roaming my body had me shuddering.

Not having any other choice, I peeked my head out of the bathroom and prayed that Nick was not in the room. To my surprise, the room dividers were already in place and my luggage was sitting on the bed. I smirked and quickly threw on my pajama bottoms and matching tank top shirt with an oversized flannel shirt before gently moving the panels and stepping into the living area.

"Thanks for getting everything set up," I said, looking at Nick. He was in a squat position, plugging in his phone before looking over his shoulder at me to chuckle.

"No problem, but you don't have to thank me for everything."

"Sorry, I just – well, I am not used to people having common courtesy for others. I've stopped relying on other people to help me out with the small things, like getting my luggage out of the car or grabbing food for me." I shrugged, walking over to the kitchen area and grabbing a bottle of water out of the fridge. I looked over at the shelf full of liquor before turning my eyes to Nick.

"You want to have a drink?" Nick asked, nodding toward the shelf as he stood up.

"No, I want to keep my head on straight tonight."

Nick cocked his head to the side in confusion. I slowly blinked and stared at him. I was terrified of embarrassing myself, but this was going to be my last night with Nick. I just wanted us both to be in our right mind so that we wouldn't have any regrets. I planned to be open to whatever happened, but I've never been this bold before. I've never cheated on anybody before either.

Bobby had been destroying my confidence bit by bit and I finally questioned if I believed our relationship was going to last. Sitting in the car covered in vomit gave me time to really think about it. The way he'd been treating me over the past few years was atrocious. I'm surprised I stayed around long enough to deal with his bullshit. Hell, I already started to plan out how I was going to break off the engagement.

Since I was alone in an intimate resort with a sexy ass stranger, why wouldn't I get a taste before we departed ways? After tomorrow, I'd never have to worry about seeing him again. If I did run into him later, it would probably be awkward, but I wasn't worried about that right now.

"Well, the last time we were alone together at night, things got a bit…interesting. I'll assume it had to do with alcohol. So, whatever happens, I want us both to have a clear mind." I finally said.

"You think something will happen between us?" Nick asked, taking a few steps toward me.

I bit onto my bottom lip and shrugged my shoulders. "Whatever happens, happens."

A sly smile spread across Nick's face for a brief moment, but it faltered. "Ashlynn, as much as I want to eat up every inch of your body, I don't want you to be ashamed of anything we may or may not do in the morning. Just think on it while I take a shower."

I nodded my head and watched him disappear behind the panel. After a few minutes, I heard the shower turn on. I rubbed the bridge of my nose and sighed. What did I want? Shit, I was so confused about what I wanted to do and I really did need to think. I noticed there was an enclosed patio attached to the villa and decided to get some fresh air.

I stepped outside and even though a snowy mountain for skiing was visible from where I was standing, it was quite toasty. The heater from inside traveled to the patio, which allowed guests to enjoy the scenic view without having to bundle up in layers.

I took a sip of water and thought about what Nick had said and realized he was right. A part of me was going to be filled with guilt if things escalated between us. Two and a half years is a long time to be with someone and I never thought that I would be lusting after another man. I am not the type of person who could purposely hurt another individual. Hell, I've spent the majority of my life trying to please others and avoiding any type of confrontation.

Then again, look where that's gotten me. So why should I give a rat's ass now? Nick has spent the past few days with me, and he's treated me ten times better than Bobby has since we've been dating. I mean to be fair, I allowed Bobby to treat me poorly and I never corrected it. I was so caught up with the idea of being in a relationship and the idea of being married that I had my eyes closed to the disrespect.

Not anymore. My eyes were wide open, and his impertinent ass had to go. I'm tired of being mistreated by the person who so-called loved me. Tonight, I was ending the chapter on me and Bobby. Being with Nick may be a one-time thing, but I was okay with that.

I walked back into the villa and towards the bathroom. My heart pounded as I stepped closer and closer to the door. I wanted Nick, even if it was just for a night. Before I could knock, Nick opened the door with nothing but a black towel. His body glistened and he smelled of Old Spice and coconut.

While I still had the courage, I slid my oversized flannel shirt down my shoulders and let it drop to the ground. The white spaghetti-strapped shirt I had on hugged my body and allowed my cleavage to sit freely. I didn't have on a bra, so my hard nipples stared at him, welcoming. The pajama bottoms sat at my waist, exposing my thick thighs. It wasn't lingerie, but by the way Nick's eyes roamed down my body, the simplicity was getting the job done.

I arched a flirtatious eyebrow at him before taking one step closer. Nick was in front of me within a blink of an eye crushing his lips against mine. His hands ran down my back and gripped my ass. I moaned as he flicked his tongue against mine and squeezed me harder.

"Fuck, Ashlynn. I've been wanting to do this since we got on the Ferris wheel in Chicago." Nick whispered against my lips.

I chuckled, "I've felt the same way. I wanted to tell you so bad to kick that bitch out of your room and stay in mine that night."

I trailed my tongue up the side of his neck and felt his dick pressing against me through the towel. I stood up on my tiptoes and nibbled on the bottom of his ear. Nick's eyes closed as he groaned before grabbing me by the back of my thighs and picking me up.

"Whoa," I screamed, wrapping my arms around the back of his neck. He held me in the air like I weighed nothing.

"I won't drop you, baby," Nick said in between kissing my neck.

"I-I know, it's just no one's ever picked me up before. Put me down if I'm too heavy, Nick. I don't want to hurt you," I stammered out.

Nick planted his lips against mine. "Lynn, you could never hurt me."

I rubbed the back of his head as I hungrily took his lips. He carried me toward the bed area and pushed down the room dividers. I laughed as I bit on his bottom lip. Nick gently planted my feet back on the ground before looking down at me.

"I want to see you — all of you baby," Nick said, grabbing his dick that was poking out of the towel.

I hesitated and stared at my feet. I knew I shouldn't be embarrassed because he clearly wanted me, but I still felt a bit uncomfortable. I had a long way to go in appreciating and loving myself, but I was determined to get there.

With shaky hands, I slowly pulled down my pajama bottoms uncovering my bare pussy. Nick groaned as I pulled my tank top over my head letting my triple D breasts fall freely. I pulled my hair out of its bun and let it fall down to my back. I squared my shoulders and placed my hands on my hips. This is who I was – I no longer would be ashamed of how I looked.

"Gotdamn Lynn," Nick muttered, stroking himself.

He pulled my head back by my hair and dipped his tongue into my mouth. I captured it with my lips and gently sucked on it. He let go of me and gently pushed me down on the bed with a smirk. Laying me on my back, he alternated between soft kisses and tender bites down my body.

My chest rose and fell rapidly as his lips made my body tingle. He moved down to the edge of the bed and planted sensual kisses along my belly. I giggled as I ran my hands through his locs.

Nick suddenly scooped my legs under his arms and wrapped them around his neck. My breath caught as he ran his tongue up my center. My back arched as he teased my clit with the brush of his tongue.

"Ni-Nick," I whimpered.

"Fuck Ashlynn, you are so fucking sweet," Nick whispered against my clit before capturing it between his lips and sucking.

My body jolted and I squirmed in his grasp as he alternated between sucking and licking my clit. I felt my body tingle and I knew I was on the verge of coming undone. Bobby nor my toys came nowhere close to Nick's tongue work.

Nick suddenly plunged his tongue and two fingers inside of me and I could no longer hold on. I grabbed the sides of his head and held him in place as I grinded my hips against his tongue. Nick moaned as I let out an orgasmic scream.

"Shit, Nick!" I cried out, trying to catch my breath. He chuckled as he laid kisses up my inner thighs. I sat up on my forearms as he stood up.

"That was the best thing I've eaten in a long time," he said, rubbing my pussy juices in his beard and licking his fingers.

"That was amazing," I giggled.

My eyes roamed down his body and my eyes widened at his hard dick pointing right at me. I licked my lips and knelt to the ground. I looked up at Nick as I slid my tongue across the tip of his head.

"Ahh, shit," he groaned.

I slowly took him into my mouth inch by inch and moaned as he hit the back of my throat. I bobbed my head back and forth, coating his length with my saliva, each pass made it easier to slide him into my mouth faster and faster. Nick's hands gripped my head as he fucked my face.

"Fuck baby," he cried through gritted teeth. "I'm about to cum."

I stared up at him as he thrusted faster and within a few minutes, my mouth was filled with his warm liquid nectar. I swallowed the sweet tangy concoction and stood on my feet. I started toward the bathroom, but Nick pulled me back toward him.

"Where are you going?" Nick asked with an arched brow.

"To clean up," I said, feeling a bit sad. I could've kicked myself for giving him head. Now I ruined the night by having things end so soon since he already nutted. I just couldn't help myself – I wanted to taste him.

"You're already done for the night?" Nick asked, looking confused.

"Uh, no, but I thought you were since…well you busted your nut."

"Baby, I was just getting started with ."

Nick pushed me back onto the bed and flipped me on my stomach. He pulled my hips up leaving my ass in the air and kept my chest flat against the mattress. I opened my mouth to ask what he was doing when I felt his tongue glide from my center to my clit.

"Oh, Nick," I groaned in the mattress.

"I just love the way you taste. So. Fucking. Sweet," he mumbled in between each suckle of my clit. He feasted on my pussy until I felt my body shudder with another climax.

"Nick, what are you doing to me?" I panted.

"Whatever you want me to do," he uttered, slapping my ass. "What would you like me to do to you now?"

"I want to feel you inside me."

"Mmm, you want me to fill you up, like this?" Nick asked, slowly inserting the head of his dick in my opening and pulling out abruptly.

"Stop teasing me baby," I groaned. I tried pushing my hips back against him, but he laughed and slapped my ass again.

"I got you baby. Stay just like that," he instructed.

After a few seconds, I felt the bed shift as he positioned himself behind me. The unwrapping of a condom came before I felt Nick glide his dick up and down my opening. He slid his dick inside of me and I instantly felt his length reaching my spot. My eyes rolled as he gave me slow teasing pumps.

"Gotdamn Ashlynn, you have some tight wet pussy."

He picked up the pace and pushed harder inside me. I met his rhythm by throwing my ass back against him earning a deliciously stinging slap to my ass. I reached back and grabbed my ankles causing Nick to curse.

"You're fucking dangerous," he leaned down and moaned in my ear.

"Good! Now fuck me harder, Nicohlas." I demanded, looking at him over my shoulder.

"Shit, keep saying my name like that and I won't be able to last too much longer."

He drove into me deeper and harder - I swear the clerk inside of the resort could hear my pleasure filled moans. In every position Nick put me in, he pressed against my G-spot causing my pussy to flood.

As soon as he put me back on my back, he pushed my knees to my chest and instructed me to grab my ankles. Once I was comfortable, he drove back into me and instantly pounded against my spot. My eyes rolled to the back of my head, and I could feel my climax approaching fast.

"Nicholas," I moaned, letting go of my ankles and digging my nails in his back.

"What did I say about you saying my name like that?" Nick whimpered, attempting to hold back his climax.

"Nicholas, baby, I'm cumming," I wailed in blissful pleasure.

"Gotdamn!" Nick yelled. He grabbed my hands and sucked on my fingers.

My body sputtered as my climax released from my body. A few seconds later, Nick cried out and I held him close to me as he shuddered. He lifted up and gazed down into my eyes before placing gentle kisses against my lips. We giggled as we caught our breaths and drifted off to sleep.

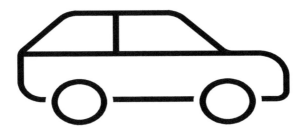

Chapter 25

Ashlynn

I rubbed my eyes as the bright morning sky peered through the curtains. A deep snore echoed behind me causing me to flinch until I realized it was Nick. I looked over my shoulder to see his peaceful face blissfully asleep and I couldn't help but smile. He made me feel so good last night. I thought Bobby felt good when we did finally have sex, but he had nothing on Nick. Bobby didn't cater to my body and my needs the way he did. I swear I'd never come as much as I had through the wee hours of the morning.

I picked up my phone and saw it was just after nine. I had two text messages and a voicemail – one text from Denice and Roshanda, my cosmetology teacher, and a voicemail from my dad. Of course, nothing from Bobby, but by the way I was feeling, I didn't give a damn.

Denice: *Girl, where the hell have you been? I haven't heard from you in two days! Are you alive over there? You better be because I'd hate to kick my best friend's ass. I'm praying for your safe travels, but bitch you better call me! I love you.*

I chuckled and made a mental note to call Denice as soon as I got dressed. I haven't spoken to her since before I left, and I had a lot to tell her and Kendra.

Roshanda: *Good morning, Ashlynn. I wanted to let you know that you have passed all of your courses, and your cosmetology license will be sent here as you asked a few weeks ago. I am very proud of you and just know if you want it, a chair is available for you at my shop. Prayers to you and your family.*

I quickly and quietly jumped out of bed and danced with excitement. I was terrified of taking my cosmetology test and I was sure I'd fail. With everything going on with planning a wedding and the abrupt call about my grandpa, I wasn't sure how I was even able to concentrate. I made another mental note to call Roshanda for more details about the opening at her salon.

Voicemail from Dad: *Hey baby girl, call me when you get a chance. I want to make sure you're okay and safe. I can't help but worry about you. P.S.: Bobby and I have come up with a few ideas for when you all take over. The boy is determined – I'm glad you got a hardworking man who loves you. Love you, call me.*

I finished listening to the voicemail and was immediately irritated – and for once not because of my dad. Bobby had been easily communicating with my dad but didn't have time to check in on me. What the fuck was his deal? It actually felt as if he was only with me to take over my dad's store. If that was the case, I was going to have his ass fired ASAP.

Not wanting to ruin my blissful morning, I wrapped the robe around my body and stepped out onto the back patio as I hit the button to Facetime Denice. Thankfully, the patio was enclosed with a heater and the cold snowy mountain wasn't affecting me much.

"I was just about to book my flight to California to find your narrow ass," Denice huffed while crossing her arms.

"Hey boo! I'm sorry I haven't called, it's been a crazy few days," I said, smiling at her.

"How crazy?" she asked, lifting both eyebrows. She held up her coffee mug and tapped giving me the signal to spill the tea.

I snorted, "Let me get Kendra on here so I don't have to repeat the full story."

Denice quietly smacked her lips before putting her cup down and turning her head. I cocked my head to the side and stared at her.

"What was that for? Please don't tell me you two have been fighting again."

"It's definitely not me! She's been acting funny lately and I mean since before you left for Cali. She doesn't like to hang out with us anymore and she's always throwing those rude ass comments toward us – especially when it comes to our weight."

I pressed my lips together and frowned. Since we all met in college, Denice and I learned that Kendra had absolutely no filter. She said whatever popped into her mind without thinking about it. It was all fun and games when we were young, but now I had to admit, it was becoming a bit much – especially since her main target has been me and Denice lately.

"I do agree that she's been heavily vocal lately when it comes to us two, but she's still our friend. We just need to have a conversation with her like adults instead of just cutting her off."

Denice sighed but nodded her head. "You're right, but off topic, what is that noise in the background? It sounds like someone's snoring."

"Shit," I grumbled as I looked over my shoulder and realized I hadn't closed the patio door all the way. Nick was dead to the world, but the world could hear his loud ass snoring. I guess I was used to the sound because I stopped noticing.

"Ashlynn Shantell Henderson, is there something you need to tell me?" Denice said, arching her eyebrows at me.

"You just going to use my full government name like that?" I chuckled. When she didn't laugh and continued to glare at me, I sighed and gave her a guilty smile.

"Like I said, it's been a long few days."

"Let me get Kendra's ass on the phone so you can tell me what the hell is going on," Denice scoffed while playfully rolling her eyes.

A few moments later, Kendra and Denice were staring at me. I shifted in my seat and pondered where I should begin. Everything had happened so fast since I last saw them Saturday morning. Saturday, my life was simple. Miserable, but simple.

Fuck it – day one, Sunday. I told them everything, except for my bulimia and everything Nick told me about his past. From my dad to my sick grandpa, to getting assaulted at the rest stop to meeting and fucking Nick, it all spilled out. I looked between both of my friends when I had finally finished.

"O.M.G," Denice squealed out. She picked up her teacup and pretended it was full. "Girl! You were not lying when you said you had a long few days."

"So, that's it? You're just going to kick Bobby to the curb like that after everything he's done for you?" Kendra snarled.

"Kendra, did you not hear what she said? Bobby has been treating her like trash," Denice shot back at her.

"I'm just saying that it's kind of fucked up to just cheat on him like that instead of talking to him first."

"This bitch," Denice mumbled with an eye roll.

"Whatever Denice! When you've been in a relationship longer than three months, then you can input your opinion."

"Girl, fuck you!"

"Enough!" I shouted, looking at both of them.

"All I'm saying is that you and Bobby have been together for a minute. Hell, y'all are in the middle of planning a wedding. You've known that man for two days and just like that you're ready to throw it all away."

Guilt washed over me as I chewed on my bottom lip.

"What does he even look like?" Kendra asked, tsking.

I stood up from my seat and quietly peeked my head through the door. Nick was still sound asleep as I turned the camera around and zoomed in on his face.

"Oh hell no!" Kendra shouted.

I ducked out of the room and ran back to the patio, not wanting to wake him up just yet.

"What? What's wrong?" I asked, staring at her in confusion.

"That's fucking Nicholas! He's at Jill's like every damn day."

"Oh, yeah he mentioned he was having an issue with his drinking, but I already know the reason why."

"Well, did he tell you everything?"

"Like what?" Denice asked.

"Like we've fooled around already," Kendra stated looking at her fingernails.

"Wh-what?" I stammered.

She shrugged her shoulders nonchalantly and gulped out of her coffee mug. A part of me wanted to believe that Kendra was lying about knowing Nick, but deep down I knew the truth. He told me himself he was battling his drinking problem and Jill's is the only good bar around Philly. If he ran into Kendra while she worked, I just knew they messed around. Kendra was sexy as fuck and knew how to get men to eat out of the palm of her hand.

"Kendra," Denice snapped, "if you are playing some type of crude joke —"

"What do I need to lie for? Look, that was the past, well technically a few weeks ago, but still the past. If you wanted to just get a taste of some other dick before you tied the knot, then hey, it's all good. I'll take your secret to the grave. You don't want to be mixing in with Nicholas like that anyway."

"Why not?" I asked, anticipation punching me in the gut.

"Well, the last time I saw him, he was in a heated argument with his friend at the bar. Apparently, his friend knew where his ex-girlfriend was — I think he said Vegas — and from the evil look on his face, I don't think he was trying to rekindle their relationship."

My mouth dropped as I stared wide-eyed at the patio door. The woman in the picture. The way Nick refused to answer me about who he was seeing in Vegas. The woman who set him up and shot him that ended with his brother getting killed. It was all making sense now – he was going to Vegas to get his revenge.

"I have to go," I said with shaky hands as I disconnected the call.

Without thinking, I stormed into the room and yanked the blanket off Nick. Bad move on my end. His dick was hard as a fucking rock and I could feel my mouth salivating. Dammit, I needed to focus. I hovered over him and shook his shoulders.

"What!" Nick snapped, throwing his hands over his eyes.

I froze when it dawned on me. This man was planning to hurt another female in ways I didn't want to imagine. He could be unhinged and on the verge of snapping. I stepped a few feet back and observed him with caution as he rubbed the sleep from his eyes.

He looked up at me and frowned. "Shit, I'm sorry Lynn. I'm not a huge morning person, but that's no excuse for yelling."

"Do you know Kendra?" I blurted out.

"Huh?"

"If you huh, you can hear!"

"Damn, Lynn what's wrong?"

"Do you know Kendra?"

"I know a few Kendra's. You're going to have to be more specific."

"From Jill's?" I said, snatching my phone out of my bathrobe pocket. Nick stepped beside me as I scrolled to a group picture of me, Denice, and Kendra.

"Hol' up, go back one picture."

"What? Why?" I asked looking at him confused.

"Just go back one."

I rolled my eyes and flicked my thumb across my phone revealing a picture of me and Bobby at one of my dad's employee dinners. Nick inhaled sharply through his nose and let out a groan. He turned away from me, shaking his head. What the hell was his problem?

"The bartender Kendra... yeah, I know her," Nick mumbled while rubbing the back of his neck. He still had his back toward me and I tried not to stare at his ass, but it was hard not to.

"Have you two fucked?" I asked, darting my eyes to the back of his head. He spun around and stared at me. Crossing my arms over my breast, I tapped my foot waiting for an answer when the muthafucka had the nerve to start laughing.

"Fuck Kendra? Hell no! She's for the streets." he snorted.

"Don't talk about my friend like that!"

"You cool with her?" Nick asked and if I wasn't mistaken, a hint of disgust and worry spread across his face.

"So, you judging people now?" I barked, feeling the need to defend her.

"I'm just saying she has a repetition. Hell, I've seen with my own eyes how she can get down at the bar. I apologize for speaking ill of her, but you should be careful of who you choose as friends."

"I thought you said you don't hurt women?" I scoffed.

"Uh, I don't. Look I didn't mean to offend but there's something about her that you need to – "

"You were going to hurt your ex-girlfriend in Vegas, weren't you?"

Nick's face scrunched up as he cocked an eyebrow. I swore a flicker of panic in his eyes, but he quickly shook his head in bewilderment.

"Who told you that?"

"Answer my question! Were you not the man who said he would never hurt a female, while he sat his black ass in my car and plotted to get his revenge on one?"

Nick's chest heaved as he took slow breaths. He slowly bent down to put on his dark gray sweats and rubbed the back of his neck. It felt like an eternity of silence as we stared at each other. He sighed and finally nodded his head yes.

I released the breath I was holding as my shoulders slumped – Kendra was right. He was heading to Vegas to hurt that woman and I was helping him get there. I was a fucking accomplice and didn't even realize it. I stumbled backward into the wall behind me.

"Lynn, I can explain."

"Explain what?" I shouted, swallowing the lump in my throat. "Kendra already told me she heard you talking about it at the bar – "

"Kendra? How the fuck -" Nick asked, interrupting me.

"Yes! I was just on Facetime with her, and she recognized you. She warned me about what she heard, and I hoped that she was lying. Guess I was wrong."

"First of all, she is a damn liar. I've never fucked her, but maybe you should ask Bobby if he has."

My mouth flew open as I glared at him. How dare he try to accuse one of my best friends of sleeping with my fiancé?

"Wow! You are a piece of work, Nicholas," I spat out his name as I began grabbing my clothes off the ground. "You get caught and instead of owning up to it, you accuse other people of doing things I know aren't true."

"I've seen Bobby at Jill's before, he and Kendra were always hugged up somewhere and always left together. Hell, she brags about how rich he is and how his girlfriend is oblivious to what they have been doing. She brags about the shit all the time once she has a few drinks in her."

I shook my head in disbelief. He was lying – he had to be. Kendra and Bobby wouldn't betray me like that, would they? I shoved my clothes into my bag as tears brimmed the edge of my eyes. My world was crumbling fast, and I needed to get the fuck away from everybody.

I zipped up my bag and wiped my eyes. I wasn't about to cry for lies. "What about the woman in Vegas?"

"I told you what she did to me and my brother! Fuck, when my friend told me where she was, I wasn't thinking straight. Yes, I wanted to get to Vegas and fuck her whole life up. Did I think about ending her life? I can admit, fuck yes – but I knew that was wrong."

"How can you think about ending someone else's life?" I shook my head. "I can't do this!"

"Lynn, baby, please. I was fucked up and holding on to hatred, but you've opened my eyes." Nick pleaded.

"Nicholas, leave me alone," I said, throwing on my thick hoodie and black leggings.

"Ashlynn, you made me remember what it was like to feel something else besides hatred. Please stay and talk to me."

I shook my head and attempted to grab my bag when Nick picked it up. I flinched back as a reflex and saw the hurt in his eyes. He dropped his shoulders and sat the bag back on the bed. We stared at each other for a few moments without uttering a word.

Shit, how did we get to this? My relaxing morning had turned into a damn shit show. I didn't know who to trust or believe anymore. Nick admitted to having evil thoughts towards his ex-girlfriend, but he said he wasn't going to go through with it. I had no idea if he was telling the truth though. And don't get me started on the accusations against Bobby and Kendra.

Nick broke eye contact with me as he turned and slowly walked into the bathroom.

"I never wanted to hurt you, nor would I lie to you," he said in a low sorrowful voice before closing the door.

I threw my bag over my shoulders before grabbing my keys and walked out of the door.

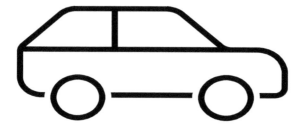

Chapter 26

Nicholas

Whoever said men don't cry never had their hearts shredded by the woman they cared for. I fucked up and now Ashlynn was gone. I didn't care that she left me stranded, but that she left me period. My hatred and need for revenge had cost me the chance of being happy again. Ashlynn was the only woman I felt truly at peace with and felt as if I could finally let go of the pain of my past. Now she was gone.

Dammit! How the fuck did I get myself into this position? No woman has ever had me acting like this, especially in such a short amount of time. Hell, not even Olivia's ass had this much of a chokehold on me. I cared for Olivia, but she had nothing on Ashlynn. I don't know how, but the connection I felt with Ashlynn was damn near instant. I mean I wasn't in love, but I wanted her to be a part of my life.

I stepped out of the bathroom and into the empty villa. The scent of her still lingered as I plopped down on the bed. I fucking missed her already. I palmed my forehead – I didn't even get her fucking number or social media accounts.

"Fuck!" I shouted, hanging my head and balling my hands into fists.

I lay on my back and stared up at the ceiling when I heard my phone ringing. I reached over to the nightstand and saw Ayzo calling me. My heart sank. I didn't know why I got my hopes up thinking Ashlynn somehow got my number.

"Yo," I answered, placing the phone on speaker and sitting it on my chest. I placed my forearm over my eyes and inhaled slowly.

"Damn, bro you good over there? Sounds like you been crying."

I grumbled a fuck you and sniffed.

"Oh shit! What happened?"

"Ashlynn left. I fucked up."

"She left? Where are y'all? What the hell happened?" Ayzo spluttered out each question.

I cleared my throat and told him everything that happened from the time we left Chicago. I didn't tell him about Lynn's sickness and starvation tactics – that wasn't any of his business. When I was done, all he could say was "gotdamn" and "shit". I nodded my head in agreement even though he couldn't see me.

"You weren't lying when you said to leave Kendra's ass alone. Hmph! She been fucking her best friend's man for Lord knows how long."

"Yup."

"And she had the nerve to make you into some type of serial killer because of your hatred toward Olivia. Even though I told you to let that shit go, but that's beside the point."

I huffed, "No you were right. I shouldn't have been plotting revenge like that. I could never take anybody's life, no matter how badly they ruined mine. On the other hand, if it wasn't for Olivia and the hatred I had toward her, I don't think I ever would have met Ashlynn. My thinking was just messed up and now I'm suffering the consequences."

"What's the plan?" Ayzo sighed. "You just going to let her go?"

I huffed out a laugh, "Man I wouldn't even know where to start to find her. I'm not going to rely on Kendra's lying ass."

"There's got to be somewhere she likes to hang out where you can meet her."

"Nah, she told me she was a homebody and didn't go out much." I rubbed down the side of my face when I remembered her dad's business. "We Got Tires!"

"Uh, come again?" Ayzo asked.

"She told me her dad owns the We Got Tires chain."

"Oh, shit fo'real? That's it then. You could probably catch up with her at one of the shops."

"I'm sure she's still heading to California and there's like seven different shops across Philly. What am I supposed to do, go visit each one of them and hope one of the employers remembers who she was?"

"Yup, that's exactly what you're going to do!" Ayzo shouted. "Women love that romantic shit. It shows how much you really care and possibly gets you out of the doghouse."

"What about her fiancé and Kendra? I honestly don't know what their deal is. I mean, Kendra didn't encourage Ashlynn to stay with me, but instead told her to leave me alone and stay with Bobby. If she and Bobby have been fucking, why would she want them to stay together and not have him all to herself?"

"Hmm, I don't know man, but it feels like more shady shit is going down. You remember how I used to roll, I can look into it for you."

"No sir. You said you were never getting caught up in that life-style again."

"I'm not. I'm just going to see what I can dig up to help get rid of both they asses so you and Ashlynn get to be together in peace. I'll be in and out before they know what hit them."

I sighed and finally agreed. I hung up the phone with Ayzo so he could handle his business. I didn't know exactly what he did, but it was dangerous enough for him to go into hiding for a bit.

I made a mental note to ask him one of these days as I booked my flight back to Philly.

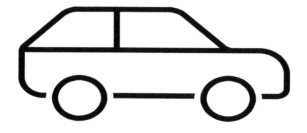

Chapter 27

Ashlynn

Maybe it was the rage fueling me, but the twelve-hour drive to California was a breeze. I took stops every few hours to use the bathroom and grab a bite to eat, but other than that, I stayed on the road.

It was after ten in the morning when I stormed out of the villa and now, I was pulling into the nursing home where my grandpa resided. I didn't want to tell my dad that I made it this late – he'd have a fit if he knew I drove for twelve hours straight. Besides, I wanted to speak with my grandpa in private first. Yes, my dad and I were working on building our relationship, but Grandpa would be easier to talk with about my plans.

I knocked on the door frame as I entered my grandpa's room. Of course, he was wide awake eating a bowl of ice cream and watching one of the Law & Order shows. His deep brown eyes lit up as he gave me a toothy grin.

"My baby girl is here!" He exclaimed, reaching his long arms out to give me a hug.

"Hey pawpaw! I've missed you," I said, enjoying his tight embrace.

"I've missed your big head ass too. Now what's this shit I hear you driving your narrow ass here all the way from Philly?"

I chuckled and plopped down on the chair next to him. "Pop, why you got to cuss me out as soon as I get here?"

"Because your dad wouldn't let me cuss your hardheaded ass out over the phone while you were driving. Where that boy at anyway?"

I knew he meant Bobby and it made me chuckle. My granddad despised Bobby from the moment he laid eyes on him. He told anyone who would listen that he seemed sneaky and to not trust him. I used to get upset with him when he went on a rant about Bobby, but now I am thinking I should've been paying attention to what he was saying.

"I'm pretty sure you know that answer Pop. You and Dad love to gossip."

"Hmph," Pop grunted with a head nod. He ate a spoonful of raspberry ice cream and turned back to his show.

"How are you feeling?" I asked during a commercial break.

"I'm old, so of course I'm tired."

I arched an eyebrow at him and folded my arms. "You know what I mean."

"Yeah, yeah, keep yo drawers on girl – I was getting to the rest. The doctors did more tests and praise the Lord, but the cancer did not spread. As a matter of fact, it's benign. Hallelujah! They don't know what a mighty God we serve."

"Granddad that's amazing!" I said jumping up and wrapping my arms around his neck.

"Hey, hey watch my ice cream," he chuckled hugging me tight. "I'm still old now and I'll be called home one day, but not right now. In the meantime, I'm going to start getting my scratch-off's and playing the lottery again because I am highly favored!"

A tear rolled down my cheek as I chuckled. He quickly swiped it away and kissed my forehead. This was excellent news and made my last twelve hours feel nonexistent. I kissed his cheek and sat back down in my chair.

"Now that I know you are going to be okay, I need some advice."

"Yes, leave that trash ass nigga and find you a man who actually cares about you."

My mouth fell open as I stared at Granddad. "Pop, it's more complicated than that."

Granddad picked up the remote and shut off the TV. He turned in his chair and gave me his undivided attention. I took a deep breath and told him everything that's happened since Dad called with the news of his health. I left out no details including my bulimia, all of the texts, and rude things Bobby told me about my weight, Nick, and my goals of not taking over the shops but starting my own business.

After I finished speaking, Granddad let out a long breath.

"I'm going to need a cigarette and a shot of brown."

"Granddad! You do not smoke or drink." I huffed out a chuckle.

"Nope, but after all of the drama you just gave me, I'm going to need one."

"C'mon, I need help. I don't even know where to start when it comes to solving all of these issues."

"Alright, first talk to your dad. He's more understanding than you think. He loves you and will not force you into something that you don't want to do. I couldn't have said that same sentence a few years ago, but he's trying to change."

I nodded. "Okay, next?"

"Next, you need to get yourself into therapy about your eating habits." He said, scolding me. "Wanting to work out and be healthy is great, but don't do it for some knuckle headed boy. Do it for yourself, shit, do whatever makes you happy! I tell ya, some of them fools wouldn't know how to appreciate what he has if it was a step-by-step manual with pictures." My grandad began to rant.

I burst into laughter, "Pops focus." I said, wiping away a tear. If I didn't interrupt him, his ass would go on and on.

"Yeah yeah! Let me see here – next, get that Bobby ass wipe the hell out of your life. I've been trying to tell your dad to not let his trifling ass be the general manager of the stores. His greedy ass cannot be trusted."

"I hear you and I am taking your advice seriously, but I have a question. Why don't you like Bobby? I mean every time he's been around you, he's been respectful and kind – not that I'm taking up for him, but just curious."

"You know I observe people, baby. That last time I flew down when your dad was opening up the fourth shop, Bobby was there. Your dad had just made him the general manager when I caught his ass over-charging folks and pocketing the change. He begged to keep his job and promised to get his act together. I sent a friend of mine to the store not even three weeks later, and that muthafucka was still doing it. The fool didn't think I had ears and eyes everywhere."

"Are you serious?" I said, scrunching up my face.

"Oh yeah! And don't get me started on all the illegal shit his ass may be dabbling in. He likes to hang around the wrong crowd and I know peer pressure can be a bitch. I've seen him socializing with a few well-known drug dealers the few times I came down to visit. I don't have any proof of what he's doing with them, but I'm sure it's no good."

"How could I have been so oblivious to what he was doing right under my damn nose? Stealing from people to satisfy his greed?" I tsked while folding my arms.

"People seem to turn a blind eye to things when they're in love. Hell, when I was younger, I fell for someone that definitely wasn't any good for me. It took me a while, but I snapped out of it."

I shook my head my head in disgust. I felt so dumb for trusting Bobby when his ass was pocketing money from hard-working paying customers this whole time. It was already hard for most people in the economy, so for him to take their money was ruthless.

I should've known he was up to no good when he always had the newest pair of Jordans or any type of technology that was trending. Our rent was well over two thousand a month plus both of us had car note payments – not to mention all of the other bills that trickled in. I was only in charge of paying my car and cell phone bills. Instead of questioning where he was getting the money, I took advantage of it by only working part-time and focusing on going to school. I wondered which of his friends was the bad influence on him. I mean I've met two of them – their names long forgotten because it was literally once years ago, and Bobby only referred to them as 'the boys' – but they seemed nice.

"I texted your dad that you were on the way to his place."

I snapped out of my train of thought and sulked as I stared at my grandpa. "Why? I don't want to inconvenience him and Ms. Linda and was going to get a hotel." Ms. Linda was my dad's longtime girl-friend. She was a widow too and was perfectly fine with not marrying again.

Smacking his lips, my granddad waved a dismissing hand at me. "I'm not going to entertain that tomfoolery. Now, my last piece of advice in regards to this Nick fella…trust your gut. If you've been with a random stranger for the past three days and not once felt uncomfortable or got the impression that he would hurt you, then what's wrong with hearing him out?"

"I don't know, it's just, Kendra knew things that – "

"Who cares what that hussy says?" he interrupted.

"Granddad!"

"Look, you know I respect women, but that girl is something else. She's broken up many happy homes and doesn't care about any-body but her damn self. Shit, she tried that mess with me, but I wasn't having it."

"What?" I coughed out.

"Oh, yeah! When she saw I wasn't a fool, she went after my friend Otis. His dumb ass got tangled up with her when I warned him not to. He gave her whatever she wanted and ended up broke and di-vorced."

"Mr. Otis? He's in his sixties!"

I couldn't believe my ears, but it was all making sense. The extravagant lifestyle Kendra lived did not match her bartender salary. I kind of had a feeling that she was getting money from men at the bar, but it never crossed my mind that she was seducing men 40 years her senior. If she tried that shit with my grandpa, then maybe Nick was right about her and Bobby messing around. The thought made my stomach clinch.

"Hey, don't let the age fool you; my friends and I still know how to spit game," he said standing up and doing a two-step dance.

I laughed and egged him on until he started laughing and sat back down.

"Granddad, I appreciate your advice, but you've given me more information than I needed to know," I chuckled as I got up from my seat.

"Alright, give me a hug." He said, walking over to me. He wrapped his arms around me and patted my back. "Get you some good therapy, practice self-love, get rid of all the negative people and thoughts, and try something new, baby girl. You don't have to settle for anything or body."

I closed my eyes and exhaled, fighting back the tears. "Thanks, Pops, I love you."

"I love you too. Now get your ass out of here so I can call Ms. Martha over."

I made a sour face and laughed as I gathered my things and left. The thought of my grandad still having sex was wild and a fact I would've been perfectly good with not knowing.

I pulled out my phone and let my dad know I was on the way. My grandad had given me so much vital information and advice that it made my head spin. Even though I was nervous, I was ready to take my life back over.

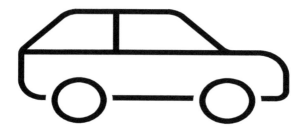

Chapter 28

Nicholas

I met Ayzo at the passenger pickup location after waiting for my bag. I hated flying, but not more than having to deal with other people at the airport. It was convenient, but mad expensive for every damn thing. Why do I have to pay four dollars for a bottle of water and three dollars for a bag of chips?

"How was your flight?" Ayzo asked, dabbing me up.

"It was a'ight. It still puzzles me that people in the back of the plane be the first ones standing up as soon as we land," I scoffed, while putting my bags in the trunk.

Ayzo laughed out loud, "Oh, don't forget the ones who be all up in what you watching because they forgot their headphones."

We got in the car and drove away from the chaos. It felt good to be back home, but I missed Ashlynn. I wondered if she made it to Cali okay. I balled my hands into fists – I should've gone with her.

"You'll see her again, don't worry."

I looked over and gave Ayzo a tight-lipped smile.

"You got it, you got it bad - when you're on the phone, hang up and you call right back!" Ayzo started singing at the top of his lungs.

"Fuck you," I snorted. I glared at him from the corner of my eyes before I busted out laughing.

"I'm just fucking with you, man. I'm glad you finally found somebody that you really care about again. Oh, shit I almost forgot," Ayzo said, reaching behind my seat. He handed me a manilla folder and dipped his chin.

"That was fast," I said, examining the folder.

He nodded, "Good news, I know where we can find Ashlynn. Bad news, Bobby is one dirty muthafucka."

"Where?" I asked, gripping the envelope.

"She lives in a townhouse in North Philly. We can wait a few days and knock on the door. Or we can catch her leaving – the main thing is we'll have to wait when she gets back from Cali."

I sighed, "Fuck, I shouldn't have let her leave on her own. Alright, what am I going to find in here?"

"You'll never guess who Bobby's best friend is," Ayzo smirked as he turned off the highway.

"Who?" I asked. I looked over at Ayzo.

He briefly looked at me before dipping his chin at the folder. I opened it and my mouth dropped open. T's black eyes stared up at me from his mugshot. I flipped to the next picture to see him and Bobby eating at a heavily guarded restaurant. T was sliding Bobby a yellow package and from the way it was shaped, it had to be full of money.

"Turns out, T is not only in the drug biz but also in the automotive business. Apparently, he has a few men stealing abandoned cars off the side of the highway and scrapping them from parts. Those lovely parts are currently being sold at and redistributed at We Got Tires, specifically the location in north Philly where Bobby spends the majority of his time."

"Gotdamn," I mumbled as I flipped through all of the pictures.

There was enough evidence here to lock Bobby and T's ass away for a minute, but it also meant that We Got Tires could be shut down. I couldn't do that to Ashlynn and her family. I had to come up with a plan to get the pair out of Ashlynn's life without jeopardizing her dad's business.

As I looked through more photos, I found one of Bobby and Kendra hugged up at the same restaurant he and T were meeting at in an earlier pic. Each photograph showed them two flirting and getting romantically closer and closer until they were kissing. The last picture in the batch showed Bobby behind a naked Kendra at Kitty's – a nude strip club - sitting next to another female.

"Damn, Kendra ass strip too?" I asked rhetorically. I glared at the image in my hands and tried to figure out who the other woman was. "I can't tell who this other woman is, bro."

"Ohhh yeah! I got another present for you – grab that folder out of the glove box." Ayzo exclaimed with a huge grin on his face as he pulled into the Airbnb he was renting.

I cocked an eyebrow before reaching forward and opening the compartment. I took out a white envelope before pulling out a stack of paperwork.

"You've got to be shitting me!" I shouted as I looked at the documents.

"That's exactly what I fucking said! That Bobby is one mutha-fucka!" Ayzo said laughing and clapping his hands on the steering wheel.

A disgusted scoff came out that turned into a throaty laugh as I stared at a copy of Bobby's marriage certificate to Charity.

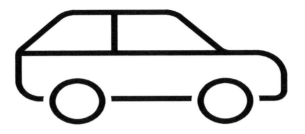

Chapter 29

Ashlynn

It felt weird sleeping in my childhood bed, but I didn't mind. After I arrived at my dad's house late last night, I ate, showered, and crashed. The long drive and drama had finally caught up to me.

I stared up at the ceiling and couldn't help but think about Nick. I hated to admit it, but I was missing him something serious. Which was completely crazy to me. How could someone I've only known for three days have such a big effect on me? A knock came at my door causing me to snap out of my trance.

"Lynn, baby, are you awake yet?" My dad asked peeking into the room.

"Yes sir, I am awake," I got out of the bed and stretched.

"Come downstairs when you get dressed. Linda is making some pancakes and eggs for breakfast."

My stomach instantly rumbled, "Thanks Dad, I'll be right down."

I snatched up a fresh pair of clothes out of my bag and headed to the bathroom. Once I was done, I followed the scent of bacon and maple down the stairs, causing my stomach to turn from a light grumble to an outright roar.

"Good morning," I said, walking into the kitchen. I walked over to Ms. Linda and gave her a hug as she handed me a plate of food. I walked to the table and sat my plate down before kissing my dad on the forehead.

"How was your drive, Lynn?" Ms. Linda asked. sitting down at the table.

"Uh, it was interesting," I said, grabbing my dad's outreached hand. In unison, we bowed our heads and said grace over our food.

"Your grandad already told me everything," Dad said, ending the prayer and pouring syrup over his pancakes.

Ms. Linda scoffed. "I swear you two are some old hens – always gossiping."

My dad waved a hand at her and looked over at me. I slowly blinked and reminded myself to be bold. It was my time to do what I wanted.

"Okay, Dad. I love you and I am very proud and grateful for all you and Granddad have done with the shops…but it's not my passion. I want to open my own salon and work for myself. I'm sorry for letting you down."

My dad reached over and squeezed my hand. "There is nothing to be sorry about. I shouldn't have tried to force the shops on you. Yes, it would be nice to keep family in the stores, but I do not want to force you into doing anything you do not want to do. I'm the one who needs to apologize for being so hard on you and not giving you a choice in your own life."

I stood up and gave my dad a tight embrace. I'd never thought I'd see the day when my dad encouraged me to follow my own dreams instead of his. Not to mention, he hasn't said anything regarding my weight or my eating habits - which I knew my Grandpa told him.

"I hope you know, you are not driving back to Philly," my dad said after we finished eating.

"What about my car?"

"We'll have it shipped. That'll usually take a few days, so I'll make sure to get you a rental."

"I'm booking you both a flight for tomorrow morning," Ms. Linda said as she gathered up our plates.

"Both?" I asked arching an eyebrow.

"Yeah, I want to make a few visits to my shops. Your grandad has been fussing about them ever since I've made Bobby the general manager."

I shifted in my seat with the mere thought of Bobby. I haven't spoken to him in days, but that was completely fine. Shit, it was actually making my decision to end things with him easier and I felt less guilty about sleeping with Nick.

Nick. I couldn't help but wonder if he was actually telling the truth about Bobby and Kendra. I mean, he told me the truth about his true intentions of going to Vegas. Granted, I had to hear it from someone else first, but he could've easily lied.

I was confused and not sure who to trust when it came to relationships. I sighed as I sat back and tried to think of something I had swept under the rug when it came to Bobby and Kendra. There have been a few times, I've seen them talking but not enough to raise suspicion.

Well, except for the way he looked at her when we were wedding dress shopping. Or the fact that he admitted to texting her without my knowledge. Okay, now that I really think about it, I was choosing to ignore the red flags waving in my face. I shook my head. At least I was opening my eyes now, and I was ready to start over and focus on myself.

"So, your granddad mentioned a young man by the name of Nick who was with you the entire trip even though you had no idea who he was."

I swallowed and nodded. I braced myself for the lecture my dad was about to give me and held my breath. When nothing happened, I slowly exhaled and observed him. My dad's face was a mixture of emotions I couldn't put my finger on.

"I'm not thrilled you spent almost forty hours in a vehicle with a complete stranger, but I am glad he was there to protect you and get you safely here. I hope I'll be able to meet him one day to thank him.

With that said, I know you have been having second thoughts of being with Bobby and just know I support whatever decision you make. If everything is still running smoothly at the shops when we get back there, and I find out that Pops was just being paranoid, he'll still be the general manager. The shops will still be under our family name, he'll just be co-owner – does that sound fair?"

I grinned and nodded. Bobby may have been a terrible boyfriend and fiancé, but I couldn't deny that he was a hard worker. Firing him just because we weren't going to be together would be childish. I'm sure we could be cordial and keep it professional.

Now if my grandpa was telling the truth about him overcharging people, his ass was gone. I'd swallow my pride and run the shops for a while until we could find an adequate replacement.

My phone buzzed with a text notification from Denice asking me to call her ASAP. I excused myself from the table and darted to my room as the phone rang for Denice.

"Hey girl, I apologize. I think I was just being paranoid," Denice sighed, answering the phone.

"What's wrong?"

"Well, you know I pass by your house on my commute to work, right?"

"Right."

"So, as I am driving, I saw that guy!"

"What guy?" My heart thumped loudly in my chest as I pressed the phone closer to my ear.

"I think you said his name was Nick, right?"

"Wh-what? How? Where?" I spewed out questions, pacing back and forth.

"He was walking to your mailbox when I was passing by. I circled the block, but he was gone when I passed by again."

I blinked several times trying to comprehend what she was telling me. How the hell did Nick know where I lived? Did he go through my purse when I wasn't paying attention? What the hell did he put in my mailbox? Heat traveled throughout my body and I felt as if I was about to pass out.

"Lynn? Are you there?" Denice asked.

I walked over to my open window and let the crisp fall air fill up my lungs and travel down my body. "Y-yeah, I'm here. Just really confused on what's going on. I mean, I never gave Nick my address."

"Do you want me to find Bobby so he could check it out?"

My face scrunched up in confusion, "What do you mean find Bobby? Isn't he at the house?"

"Unless y'all have a third car I don't know about, I haven't seen his car parked out front since you left."

What the hell? I know Bobby worked long hours at the shops, but Denice has always seen his car when she was leaving for work or returning home. It's not like we had a garage for him to park in.

"Can I ask you a question Dee?"

"Shoot."

"Do you think Bobby and Kendra have been fucking around and he's been with her since I left?"

She exhaled, "I don't have physical proof, but I've been having a funny feeling about them two for a while. I didn't want to ruin your dream of getting married or put a strain on our friendship."

"Thanks for being honest with me Dee. It felt like something was up with them too, but I turned a blind eye to it. Nick told me he's seen the both of them together at Jill's flirting. I didn't believe him at first, but the look on his face told me what I already knew – deep down."

"I'm sorry boo. Ever since you left, her ass has been M.I.A. When you called us yesterday, that was the first time I've spoken to or seen her since we went wedding dress shopping. I would be more shocked if she wasn't fucking him. Look I can grab whatever it was out of the mailbox and Facetime you."

"Okay, but please be careful."

I didn't think Nick would do anything to hurt me, but I didn't want my best friend to risk getting hurt. A few seconds later, Dee was on my screen walking toward my townhouse. She walked toward the mailbox – which was full of letters and ads. It seemed like an eternity, but Dee finally made it back to her car and had the camera positioned so I could see the envelope.

I took a deep breath as she opened it and my eyes widened in horror.

"Well, I guess that answers the questions about Bobby and Kendra," Denice said, holding the photo in her hand.

It was a picture of Kendra and Bobby wrapped up in each other's arms at Jill's, kissing passionately. Before I knew it, Denice had flipped to another picture of Bobby. This time he was leaving another woman's apartment – his arm wrapped around her waist with his tongue in her mouth.

"Bobby, that fucking slut," Denice said, slamming the pictures down on the passenger seat. "Oh shit, Lynn, there's a note." She picked up the piece of paper and read it out loud.

All I want is Ashlynn. Leave her alone because you don't deserve her! PS, I know what you are doing to her family's business – it'd be wise to leave, or things are going to get ugly.

What the fuck?

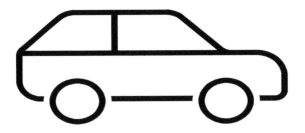

Chapter 30

Ashlynn

After finally convincing my dad to keep his flight for the following day, I was on the first flight back to Philly. I'd be back home by five in the evening which is perfect timing. Denice would be off work so she could pick me up at the airport, while Bobby would still be at the shop for another hour.

Seeing him cheat with not one, but two different women had me beyond pissed off. All of the late hours at the shop or pickup games at the rec were all a damn front. And Kendra! That bitch had been smiling in my face and helping me plan my wedding while the whole time she was fucking him!

I sat back in my seat and tried to calm my nerves. I had jumped on the plane with pure emotion and had no actual plan in place. I couldn't kick Bobby out because technically the place was his. It was under his name, and I couldn't afford to pay the mortgage on it. Besides, I wouldn't even want to stay there – too many bad memories and he probably fucked one of his girlfriends there.

"Ladies and gentlemen, we are beginning to descend and should be landing in the next fifteen minutes. The weather is currently 52 degrees with partly sunny skies. We want to thank you for flying with us and we hope you have a wonderful rest of the day." the pilot announced over the intercom.

I was overcome with anxiety as the plane descended. I decided to confront Bobby and Kendra first — just rip off that band-aid. Then I was going to try and find Nick. I owed him an apology and wanted to know whatever it was he knew about Bobby, especially if it had anything to do with my father's business.

"I'm so glad you made it safely," Denice said hugging me at the pickup location. I missed my friend and was happy to see her.

"Here's the plan," I started after we drove off, "I am going to talk to Bobby and Kendra first – "

"Good because I got my Vaseline and good shoes in the back," Denice interrupted.

"No, no fighting. I want this to be as smooth as possible. Now if anybody starts swinging, then we bust out the Vaseline."

Denice let out an exasperated breath before agreeing. I patted her shoulder and told her I loved her for caring. As much as I wanted to ram my foot up Kendra's ass and dick stomp Bobby, neither one of them was worth that type of energy. If they wanted to be together, then they could. I was unhappy and should've left both of those relationships a long time ago.

Denice and I chatted some more as I went into more details about what happened on my mini road trip with Nick. I still did not tell her about his past since it wasn't my story to tell, but I did confess to her about what I was doing to myself. We had to pull over for a few minutes as we cried and hugged.

Forcing my body into starvation and making myself vomit because of my insecurities and low self-esteem made me feel ashamed of myself. I hated how I looked and tried to force myself to change in an unhealthy way. I held on to that secret for so long and was afraid of being judged. My mindset was only focused on getting thinner – not for myself, not to be healthy, but only for other people to accept me.

Spending time with Nick and my own thoughts made me aware of how harmful my actions and current state of mind were. I was willing to purge my body on a daily basis for people to love me. I should've been loving myself. I realized talking about it to the ones I loved the most made me feel better. I was still seeking professional help, but it was nice to know that I had support as I took the journey.

We finally pulled into my neighborhood and dread came over me. I didn't want to go in just yet so I instructed Denice to park on the side of the street. She had already given me the blessing of moving into her spare bedroom until I found a place of my own, even though I didn't want to inconvenience her like that. I promised to be out of her hair in a few weeks. Besides, I needed to relearn who I was on my own.

"We can grab just a few things for now and hire movers to get the rest of your things," Denice stated, giving me an encouraging smile.

I smiled back at her and nodded, feeling grateful to have a true friend like Denice. My mind was still wondering what I should do next when I swung the car door open, hitting someone in the gut.

"Oh shit!" I gasped, jumping out of the car.

The person was doubled over holding their stomach as they let out a groan. They had on a black sweater with the hood up, but by the looks of their big hands he was definitely a man.

"I am so sorry! I was not paying attention to what I was doing. Fuck, I hope I didn't hurt you too bad," I explained, dropping down next to him and rubbing my hand down his back.

To my surprise, he started to chuckle. I looked up at Denice who was staring down at the man, just as puzzled. I started to stand up right when he placed his hand on my thigh.

"I told you, you could never hurt me," his low voice whispered.

My breath caught and my heart pounded so loud against my chest, I thought Denice could hear it. I ran my hand up his back and pulled down the hood of his sweater. Nick's warm honey eyes stared back at me, and a smirk was planted on his face.

I reared my hand back and slapped him. Denice gasped as his head snapped to the side. I pulled the neckline of his sweater toward me and smashed my lips against his. He hungrily accepted and kissed me back as he wrapped his arms around me.

"Damn, did you have to slap him?" Denice chuckled as she leaned against the car facing away from us.

Nick pulled back and laughed, "Yeah, did you have to slap me?"

"I slapped you because how the hell did you find out where I lived?"

"I have a friend who's good at getting information," Nick shrugged.

"Oh no you don't! If we are going to make this work, then you have to be honest with me."

"I can't have someone go Dora on you like you did my wallet?" he asked with an arched brow.

Denice looked over her shoulder, "Go Dora?"

"Go exploring," we said in unison before looking at each other and laughing.

"Oh lawd, he's just as goofy as you," Denice chuckled with a head shake.

Our laughter dwindled and Nick grabbed my hands, standing me up. He rested his forehead against mine as he slowly blinked.

"I fucking missed you," he whispered.

"It's only been a day since you last saw me," I retorted.

"It felt like an eternity – I didn't think I'd ever get the chance to see you again."

My body tingled all over as his lips brushed against mine. I wanted to pull him into the house and ravish him on the bed I once shared with Bobby. Nothing like leaving my final fuck you on his favorite comforter set.

"I hate to break up the reunion, but it's kind of cold out here," Denice commented.

"Sorry, Dee. C'mon, let's go inside."

"Yes, we have a lot to talk about," Nick said, intwining his finger with mine.

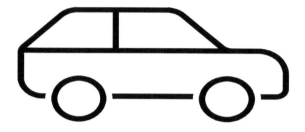

Chapter 31

Nicholas

I was thrilled Ashlynn was back - it was luck that I ran into her. I was stopping by her place to have a chat with Bobby, but instead, I got the wind knocked out of me by the woman who was stealing my heart. I had no idea where we stood, but I was by her side with whatever decision she made.

I grabbed her by the waist and pulled her into me. Her ass rubbed against my groin as I squeezed her and kissed the side of her neck. She tilted her head back to look up at me and smiled.

"Don't start anything you're not going to finish," she whispered.

I arched an eyebrow at her, "Denice, make yourself comfortable, we'll be right back."

Ashlynn gave me a confused look before I scooped her legs into my arms and carried her up the stairs. Denice laughed and told us she was grabbing a bite to eat and would be back later. She shouted a "have fun" before the door clicked closed. Ashlynn flicked her tongue against my ear as I carried her to the first room from the stairs.

I sat her down on the full-size bed and pulled her hoodie over her head. She simultaneously unbuckled my pants and shoved them down to my ankles. Before I could unhook her bra, she had my dick out. Her eyes seductively watched me as she planted teasingly kisses up my shaft. I groaned as she fully took me into her mouth.

"No fair, I was supposed to be pleasing you," I moaned as her tongue swirled around the tip of my dick. She giggled and the vibrations had my toes curling.

I pulled her head back, not wanting to bust yet, and pushed her on her back. I pulled down her leggings and panties and rubbed my thumb against her clit. She moaned as I leaned down and flicked her nipple with my tongue.

I finished getting undressed and laid down next to her on the bed. I pulled her on top of me as I continued to squeeze and suck on her breasts.

"Sit on my face, baby" I demanded while nibbling on her nipples.

"Wh-what? No, I can't do that. I'm going to smother you."

I slapped her ass, "Get your sexy ass on my face, now!"

She sat on her knees as she wrapped her arms around her belly. I watched as she chewed on her bottom lip nervously.

"Baby," I said sitting up on my forearms, "you are not going to hurt me. I just want your sweet pussy juice coated on my face."

She smirked and climbed on top of me. She positioned each of her knees along the sides of my head allowing me full access to her sex. I opened her lips and guided my tongue directly on her clit. I watched with awe as she squirmed. I ran my hands up her body and slapped her ass as she grinded against my lips.

"Mmhmm, ride my face," I moaned as I sucked her clit.

She suddenly got up and moved down the bed. She gripped my dick and rubbed it against her soaked opening. I held my breath as she slid her pussy down onto my length. I instantly moaned feeling her pussy squeeze my dick.

"Fuck," she whimpered. I held on to her hips as she bounced up and down on me. Without breaking her stride, she twisted around into a reverse cowgirl.

"Gotdamn baby!" The way her ass jiggled each time it slapped against me had me gripping the sheets.

"You fucking like that?" she moaned, looking back at me.

The sight of her ass, her curvy body, and her beautiful face had my stomach fluttering and my balls tightening. I reached up and pulled her hair back pressing my lips against her ear. "You are fucking dangerous."

She laughed wiggling her head out of my grip. Before I could reach for her again, she bent down and grabbed my ankles giving me full view of her ass. Her pussy swallowed up my dick and I could feel my nut brewing in my lower abdomen.

"Fuck, Nick!" She whimpered as her body shook. A wave of her juices came crashing down on my dick causing my own orgasm to release. A held on to her hips as I gave her one final thrust before busting my nut.

We lay there for a few minutes and as we caught our breaths. I wasn't sure what was next for the both of us, but I knew I one thing – I wasn't going to let her go.

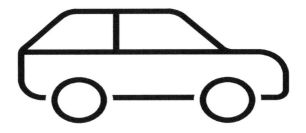

Chapter 32

Ashlynn

D enice came back with a few boxes of pizza and some bottled waters. She gave us both a knowing look before shaking her head and chuckling. After we had our fill and started to clean up, my phone started ringing. I assumed it was my dad checking in, but I was shocked to see Bobby calling.

"Wow," I said out loud as I shook my head. I hadn't spoken to him since he sent me those lovely emojis two days ago.

"Answer it bae. Find out where he is for me," Nick said, rubbing my arm.

Denice's eyebrows rose and she gave me a sly smile followed by a wink. I snickered and rolled my eyes as I answered the phone.

"What's up?"

"Lynn baby what are you doing? Have you made it to Cali yet?"

I started to tell him I had made it back when Nick shook his head. I cocked an eyebrow at him but played along. "Uh, the trip is okay. I'm in Vegas now and should be in Cali by tomorrow."

"Oh, okay that's good. Remember about your wedding dress - don't spend all of your money on gambling and food," he laughed in my ear.

I balled my hands into fists as I opened my mouth to cuss him out when I felt Nick wrap an arm around my waist. He kissed the back of my neck as he snuggled his nose against me. He tilted my head to the side and gave me a quick kiss and winked.

I smiled before clearing my throat, "Anyway, what are you doing?"

"Oh, just at the house about to get ready for bed – I've had a long day at the shop."

I rolled my eyes at his blatant lie. "Oh, you poor baby. Well, get some rest and I'll call you tomorrow when I get to Dad's house."

"Yes, make sure you call me as soon as you get there. I can't wait for us to take over the shops – I have so many great ideas to have us both financially comfortable."

"I can't wait to hear them," I lied. I noticed how Nick stiffened next to me and I began to worry. "Good night Bobby."

"Night Lynn, love yah."

Before I could say anything else, he disconnected the line. Nick exhaled loudly as he sat down on the stool.

"That man is a piece of work," Denice said, pouring us a glass of wine, sat it on the counter in front of us, and walking to the bathroom.

"You have no idea," Nick grumbled, motioning for me to sit down next to him.

"What do you mean?" I asked looking at him puzzled.

"Well," he started when a knock came at the door.

"Hold that thought."

I got out of my seat and headed toward the front door. Nick trailed behind and quickly grabbed the door handle before I could. He briefly checked through the peephole before swinging the door open and motioning for someone to come in.

A tall slightly muscular man with thick brown curly hair walked into the house. He gave Nicholas a quick dab before turning to me and smiling.

"Damn Nicholas, I see why you were acting the way you were. Baby girl is fine," he said reaching over and grabbing my hand. He briefly kissed it before Nick slapped the back of his head.

"Bro chill out!" Nick scowled.

"I meant no offense," the man said smiling and placing his hand on his chest. "I'm Ayzo, Nick's best friend."

"Oh, nice to meet you," I laughed.

"He's the reason I knew where to find you," Nick stated.

"Ah! So I owe you a jab to the gut too," I scoffed, placing my hands on my hips.

He rubbed the side of his smooth face and nervously chuckled. I heard the bathroom door open and heard Denice approaching us. The smile on Ayzo's face faltered as he stared past me.

"H-hi," Denice said.

"Hey," Ayzo said looking down and shoving his hands in his pockets.

I looked between them in confusion. "Uh, have y'all met before?"

Denice shifted her weight onto her other foot. "Something like that. We'll talk later."

I nodded at her and noticed a look of sadness crossed along Ayzo's face as he continued to stare at her. I wanted to know now, but I didn't want to pry.

Ayzo opened his mouth to say something, but instead cleared his throat. "Nicholas, what's the plan to take down Bobby?"

"Huh? What do you mean take down Bobby? I thought I could just confront him about him and Kendra. He can still be the manager of the shops – "

"Lynn, baby, it's much deeper than him just having an affair," Nick said looking down at me.

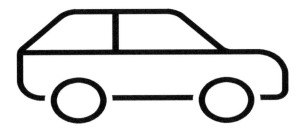

Chapter 33

Nicholas

I rubbed Ashlynn's back as she flipped through pictures of Bobby and the documents Ayzo had gathered. She was beyond pissed when she found out he was not only jeopardizing her father's business, but that he was actually already married.

"I can't believe that son of a bitch has been playing me this whole damn time," Ashlynn said, slamming the papers on the coffee table.

"It's okay baby. We got something for his ass."

"What's the plan?" Denice asked, folding her arms.

"Right now, Bobby has no idea that you know all of his dirty secrets. All we have to do is find out where he is and ambush him," I said.

Ashlynn shook her head, "I don't know – do you think he's going to just give up that easily? I mean, his dream is to take over my family's business for good. Right now, he's only working with that T guy out of one shop. Imagine what he could do if he had all five shops running the same."

"We need to set him up – make him believe that T doesn't trust his ass anymore," Ayzo said.

"How do we do that?" Ashlynn said, scrunching up her eyebrows.

"One thing T hates is a talker. He despises someone who can't keep their mouth shut by telling someone's secrets," I explained, looking at her.

"Lucky for Mr. Bobby, he has two women who don't know how to keep their mouths shut," Ayzo chuckled.

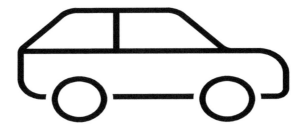

Chapter 34

Ashlynn

Butterflies filled my stomach as I sat at the bar. It was a quarter till six and Kendra was not due to start her shift at Jill's until seven. It took me a few days, but I finally got Bobby to agree to meet me at the bar. He kept insisting we meet at the house since he thought I just made it back from Cali, but I lied and told him I wanted to go out and celebrate my grandad's health.

Ayzo walked in and headed toward the pool table with one of T's closest friends. We briefly made ete contact and he dipped his chin, acknowledging me. We had a pretty solid plan in place, but I was still nervous. I checked my phone and realized fifteen minutes had gone by – shocker, Bobby was late. My phone buzzed with a text notification.

Nick: *When this is done, I am going to take you back to my room and suck your clit until you see stars.*

"Sorry I was late sweetheart, I got caught up with some business at one of the shops," Bobby said, sitting next to me.

I jumped from his startling entrance and quickly closed the message while displaying a phony smile, "It's okay babe."

He looked me up and down and I could've sworn he grimaced. "You must not plan on going wedding dress shopping soon."

I balled my hands into fists before closing my eyes and taking a breath. I only had to deal with his ass a few more minutes before he was out of my life for good. I cleared my throat and proceeded to gather the envelope from my purse. Right on cue, Kendra walked into the bar and headed toward the employee area.

I watched as Bobby's eyes followed her before he broke his trance. "What's that?" he asked, nodding toward the envelope.

"Hmm? Oh, I have no idea. It was in the mailbox when I got in a few hours ago." I handed him the packet and sipped on my drink.

"Right, it totally slipped my mind to check the mailbox. I bet it was full as hell," Bobby said, opening the envelope. "Sorry about not picking you up from the airport, you know how work gets."

I pressed my lips together into a grin before turning my attention to the tv in front of me. I wasn't paying attention to what was on, but I needed to keep up the act. The employee door swung open and Kendra came walking out.

"Look who's back!" she squealed, pouring herself a shot. "What's up Bobby?"

Bobby didn't say a word, but by the way his nostrils were flaring, I could tell he was not happy and it was taking everything in me not to laugh. My phone buzzed with another message from Nick.

Nick: *She's about to walk in*

I quickly scanned the message before refocusing back on Kendra. "Girl I am so glad to be back, that drive was crazy."

"I bet," she said sarcastically with an arched eyebrow.

Before I could respond, Bobby jumped up from his seat. "Yo, I need to talk to you, now!"

"Wh-what?" Kendra stammered, looking at him.

"Bobby, baby, what's going on?" I asked.

The door chimed, indicating someone had walked in. Kendra's eyes widened as she stared past me and at the door.

"So, this is your mistress?" a female voice snapped from behind me.

Bobby and I whirled around to see a woman wearing a black jumpsuit and matching black Nike's with long red hair. Her dark brown eyes glared at me and then at Bobby.

"Charity, what the fuck are you doing here?" Bobby whispered in a snarl.

"What am I doing here? What the hell are you doing here? You told me you were going to be working late at the office, not with this chunky ass girl."

I rolled my eyes.

"Baby, I told you, she's my boss's daughter and –"

"Wow!" I said as loud as I could while standing up. "I'm just your boss's daughter? We aren't engaged now?"

Eyes were focused on us throughout the bar, including T's friend that was still at the pool table with Ayzo. He squinted his eye and realized it was Bobby.

"How the fuck are you engaged when you are already married?" Charity snarled. She shot her eyes at Kendra and threw up her hands. "Kendra, what the fuck? Oh, I get it! You two were trying to change the plans."

"Charity, baby, calm down," Kendra soothed, walking toward her.

"Don't give me that shit! Y'all two have been trying to boot me out for a while now. You're friends with her ass and Bobby's fucking her – easy access to her dad. Y'all were going to cut me out of the money and take over the shops without me." Charity yelled, balling her hands into fists.

"Charity, shut the fuck up!" Bobby hissed.

"No! I want my cut of the money – I've done my part."

"What is she talking about?" I asked, wanting Charity to keep talking. I looked out the corner of my eyes and the man with Ayzo had his phone subtly pointed toward us. I assumed he was recording. "I need to know what's going on or I am leaving."

"Baby wait," Bobby pled. "Let me just talk to you privately so I can explain everything."

Charity scoffed, "so you're calling your boss's daughter 'baby'? I can't believe I waited this long to divorce your trifling ass. I can't believe I let you two convince me of this stupid plan."

"Charity, you need to calm down fo'real or you're going to fuck up everything," Kendra said in a low voice. She had moved next to her and was rubbing her hand down her back.

"Fuck you Kendra! You and Bobby were going to cut me out, don't try to deny it. Yall have been spending time together without me even though you promised not to." She yelled. pushing Kendra.

My jaw hung open. What kind of freaky shit were they all on? What I picked up so far was that Bobby was married to Charity when they decided to invite Kendra into their bedroom. I quietly chuckled as I took a sip of my drink. All I needed was some popcorn because this was the type of shit I'd only seen in movies.

"Charity! Don't say another fucking word," Bobby growled, grabbing her by the arm. He finally noticed the man in the corner moving closer and attempted to pull her toward the door.

She snatched her arm away and jabbed him in the chest, "You only married me so you could use me like I was your personal fucking prostitute! Had me fucking T and a few of his friends in exchange for him using the shop for all of those damn parts he -,"

Panic crossed Kendra's face as she recognized the man with Ayzo who was now sneering. "You stupid bitch – shut up!" Kendra yelled, pushing her to the ground.

Before I knew it, Charity was back on her feet and punched Kendra square in the nose, sending her flying into the bar stools next to me. I jumped back and moved to the side as Bobby ran over to help Kendra up. Charity picked up one of the bar stools and crashed it down on his back.

"Bitch!" he yelled out in pain.

"I got your bitch!" Charity yelled, slamming the stool down again. "Did you think you were going to fuck me over? I don't fucking think so!"

"Y'all got to go. Now!" Ms. Jill shouted, storming in from the back room with her shotgun.

Bobby slowly stood up with a groan before grabbing his phone and the documents and storming out of the bar. The man who was friends with T slipped his phone back into his pocket before nodding his head toward Ayzo and following Bobby out the door.

Charity glared at me and then at Kendra before turning and stomping out of the bar. Kendra averted her gaze before shutting her eyes and intaking a sharp breath. She opened her mouth to speak, but I shook my head. I grabbed one of the pictures of her and Bobby together from my back pocket and shoved it in her chest.

"I enjoyed the show. I have to admit though, you almost had me with the whole 'don't throw away your relationship for some stranger' speech when this whole time you were fucking Bobby. Hell, you knew he was already married and yet you went wedding dress shopping with me."

Kendra scoffed and rolled her eyes, "Charity and I have been friends for a long time, and she let me share Bobby with her. It was my idea to have Bobby seduce you so that we could profit from your dad's shops."

I pursed my lips and squinted at her, "You tried to seduce my granddad first, but when he didn't budge, y'all sent Bobby after me."

"It's easier to manipulate timid females. Did you think I wanted to be friends with you back in college? When you told me who your family was, I thought it would be easy to get your granddad to fuck, but his old ass wasn't having it. So, I started to hang out with you more to make you think we were best friends."

I balled my hands into fists when I felt a hand wrap around my waist. Kendra's eyes bulged as her smirk disappeared.

"Well, isn't she a miserable jealous mess?" Nick asked before kissing the top of my forehead.

I cocked my head to the side and wrinkled my nose. "She is, isn't she?"

Kendra's jaw clenched as she bumped past us and out of the front door.

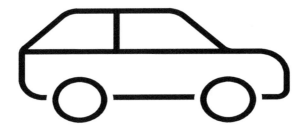

Chapter 35

Nicholas

I stared at Ashlynn's naked body lying next to me in bed. We had spent all night celebrating her for retrieving her cosmetology license and securing her chair at Unique's Salon. Even though her dream was to start up her own business, she wanted to get in as much practice and recognition before she took that next step.

It had been a few weeks since we got all of her stuff from her ex's townhouse and he was still calling her phone, begging her to take him back. She knew his ass was desperate since her dad fired him and T exiled his ass from doing any type of business with him or his other associates.

Ashlynn yawed as she fluttered her eyes open. I ran my hand down her face and kissed her forehead.

"Mmm, good morning. Are you ready for today?"

"Not really, but I know it's time," I said sitting up.

I had made the decision to go back to my house. I hadn't stepped foot in there in over a year. I was scared of being overwhelmed with grief, but with Ashlynn by my side I knew I'd be able to get through it.

I had reached out to the realtor, and they were going to be able to get my house back on the market once they fixed a few things. The front room where the shooting happened still had visible bullet holes and the house needed a new coat of paint. I suggested they painted everything a new color to mark a new beginning.

After we got dressed and grabbed a quick breakfast, we were in my truck. Ashlynn rubbed my shoulder as I drove down the highway and pulled into the cul-de-sac. I parked and turned off the car.

"You and Garrett picked out a beautiful home," Ashlynn said staring, out the window.

"Yeah, I almost forgot how nice and quiet it was here."

I stepped out of the car and walked up the pathway to the door with Ashlynn at my side. I wanted to make sure the carpet was taken out as requested before I opened the door. I peeked in and was relieved that it was gone. I took in a sharp breath before unlocking the door with my key.

My eyes immediately landed on the spot where I held Garrett as he died. I froze as my heart pounded. My life was turned upside down in the worst possible way. I lost my brother and the woman I thought I was going to marry. I was slowly killing myself by numbing my emotions with alcohol and sex – clearly on the verge of a mental breakdown.

I turned to religion like Garrett asked me to do many times before he died. I wanted to follow his final wishes and hoped in the process I'd get some answers for why things turned out the way they did, but my heart was still hardened for vengeance.

I didn't want to hear or try to understand, nor did I really care about what the Bible was trying to tell me. My mind was focused on plotting to hurt the woman who hurt me the most.

I exhaled and walked deeper into the room. I knelt down and placed my hand on the ground as tears welled my eyes. God allowed me to get thrown off the bus. I was stranded in an unknown place with no one and nothing around but my own thoughts. Then I met Ashlynn. I had no idea at first why I was drawn to her when I spent the last two years pushing others away.

I chuckled as I wiped away the tears. Ashlynn knelt next to me as I looked at her and smiled.

"What's so funny?" she asked, arching an eyebrow.

"You thought I was saving you when we met at that rest stop, when the whole time, it was you that saved me. I was on a path of self-destruction, not caring who I hurt along the way. I showed you my vulnerability but instead of judging me, you showed me kindness and sympathy."

Ashlynn placed her forehead against mine as she rubbed the back of my head. I closed my eyes and let the tears stream down my face. All of the hurt, anger, and hatred that I held on to, dissolved. I titled my head and looked around the house. A mixture of sadness and joy filled my chest. Yes, the house had a very painful memory, but it also held the treasured moments I shared with my brother.

My eyes landed on my brother's room and a lump swelled in my throat. I slowly stood as I stared at the bedroom door. Ashlynn grabbed my hand and squeezed as she lead me to the room. With the help of the moving crew, all of his belongings were packed up and sent out to local shelters and goodwill facilities leaving an empty room. I didn't need to hold on to all of his things when I knew there were individuals who needed it more. Besides, the only thing I wanted to keep was one of his favorite bracelets that had Psalms 27 inscribed.

I never thought I'd be able to step back in this house let alone Garrett's room, but here I was. I had to admit, though, it felt good. A part of me was finally accepting his death and stepping foot into this house was the closure I needed. I still had a long road ahead of me when it came to properly grieving, but I was ready to start.

We sat there for a few more moments before I gently pulled Ashlynn toward me and kissed her lips. "C'mon, let's go home."

Epilogue

Denice — One Month Later

I gripped the rail on the front patio as I closed my eyes. The cool breeze brushed past me causing a delicious chill to graze my nipples. It was late November and while it was cold as hell, I didn't mind. Fall and winter were my two favorite seasons.

I sipped on my glass of wine as I stared out at the city skyline. I was dragged out of my comfortable house to have a friend's night with Ashlynn, Nick, and – ugh - Ayzo. Why did he have to be Nick's best friend? I thought I left his ass back in Chicago eight years ago. I never thought I'd see Ayzo's face again, but here he was. Fucking ghost of Christmas past.

"So are you going to just pretend that I don't exist," a deep voice said behind me.

I dropped my head back and rolled my eyes before turning around. I leaned against the rail and folded my arms against my chest. Ayzo stood before me with his hands in his pockets. His full curly hair had grown since I last saw him when I was sixteen. The curly locs used to sit just past his eyes, now the tight coils flowed freely at his shoulders. His slim body was fit and muscular and his once baby face had transformed into a sexy ass man.

I shook my head and cleared my throat. "You don't exist to me. I thought you would have gotten the hint since I have yet to acknowledge your presence longer than necessary."

"C'mon Dee don't be like that."

"It's Denice! Only my friends can call me Dee."

"I was your friend," Ayzo said walking toward me. He stopped less than a foot away and pierced his honey eyes into mine. The scent of his cologne wasn't strong, but still intoxicating. "I mean, we were becoming more than just friends."

Ayzo brushed his thumb along my bottom lip and my body shivered.

"T-that was a long time ago. Besides, it was never supposed to happen – we were young and dumb…. just forget it ever happened," I snapped, moving past him.

Memories of us flashed through my mind as I headed back inside. The stealthy glide up my thigh burned in my memory. Rough timid yet curious fingers traced outside of my panties sending electricity up my spine. Ayzo's soft lips pressed against my neck as my boyfriend called my phone for the third time. He had no idea what his best friend and girlfriend were up to.

I looked over my shoulder and Ayzo's eyes locked with mine. The longing look on his face let me know that he was thinking about that night too. Dammit, why did he come back? I shook my head. Maybe he was going to be leaving again soon. All I had to do was stay clear of him. That shouldn't be hard.

Ayzo flicked his tongue across his bottom lip as his eyes roamed down my body. Once his eyes met mine again, a panty-dropping grin spread across his face. Fuck, this was going to be harder than I thought.

Denice and Ayzo will return in Book Two: Their Best Friends

Acknowledgments

Let me start off by thanking God. He put the passion of reading and writing into my heart ever since I was a little girl.

Next, I'd like to thank my wonderful husband, Damion, for putting up with me, especially during my brainstorming process. Thank you for believing in me and encouraging me to keep going when I felt like giving up.

I'd like to thank my editor, Chonise Bass, who transformed my rough draft into this beautiful masterpiece. The hard work and dedication to my manuscript was nothing short of amazing!

I'd like to thank my ARC team for helping me get my story out into the world! Thank you for signing up and supporting an indie author.

Thank you to previous indie authors who've shared their tips and advice to self-publishing. Without y'all, my manuscript would still be just an outline sitting on my desktop.

 Last but not least, I'd like to thank you, reader, for reading my story. I hope you enjoyed it.

😊 God Bless!

About the Author

I'd like to take the time to introduce myself. My name is Jessica but as you can see, I write under the pen name J.D. Southwell. I was born and raised in DFW, TX and I've always enjoyed reading ever since I was a little girl. Unlike most kids growing up, I spent the majority of my time at my local library. I eventually found my love of Romance and Mystery books.

I started writing my own stories when I realized what I wanted to read hadn't been written yet. I started my self-publishing journey writing children's books. *(Amelia and Andrew Learn to Pray, Love One Another, and Don't Be Afraid, Grace)*

Once I got the hang of self-publishing, I wrote and published my first book, *Dating is Ghetto*: an erotic anthology novella.

After a year, I started to outline 40hrs With A Stranger. And here we are today!

I plan on writing more and hope that you sign up for my

newsletter for my next project, Their Best Friends. (Book 2 of this series, Its A Vibe)

If you've enjoyed this story, please leave me a review and share this story with a friend. Feel free to follow me on Instagram and/or Tiktok 😊

www.jbookcollections.com

email: jd.southwell@outlook.com

Instagram: @jdsouthwells

Tiktok: @jdsouthwell

Milton Keynes UK
Ingram Content Group UK Ltd.
UKHW041821140224
437823UK00001B/56